10 Regiment Studios

Free-to-Read or Buy-to-Binge

10REGIMENT.COM

presents…

Fortnite Battle Royale

The next evolution

Volume 1

(An unofficial Fortnite story)

Written by: A.I. James

10 Regiment Website

10 Regiment Studios specialize in tactical stories which also include superhero elements at times.

10 Regiment Studios has two series:

- Fortnite Battle Royale: Stories of gamers deploying inside the world of Fortnite Battle Royale using 10 Regiment's M.I.S.T. Pods technology.

- Bravo Two Eleven: This is our own original storyline about characters who don't know they exist inside a computer game and the game developers have no idea how every change or update they publish impacts the characters and the world inside the game. This series blends the best of games like Fortnite and Call of Duty with the magic and superpowers from Marvel. The M.I.S.T. books are an ongoing series filled with action packed mission deployments and bonus features. The Bravo Two Eleven Origins novel is a completed story with deeper character development and storylines that follows the character's journey from school students to elite agents. The first three stories within the book, Bravo Two Eleven M.I.S.T. Season 1 are available at the back of this book as free bonus features for your reading pleasure.

Join the free Agent List if you want to know when a new book is coming and if you want to get one free randomly selected story from every new Bravo Two Eleven M.I.S.T. book to beta test read before it is published. Give feedback to the author and help guide the direction of the series. If you sign up now, you'll get one story from Bravo Two Eleven, M.I.S.T. Season 1 within the first 72 hours of becoming an agent. 10 Regiment Studios also has a Free-to-Read or Buy-to-Binge mission. To find out more, go to:

www.10regiment.com

Glossary

A quick word on the 10 Regiment Studios terminology. We've coined words for you to recognize what is happening on the battlefield without having to lose pacing by explaining every shot. We also use capitals to emphasize yelling, sudden or violent actions. This style is not a typo. It is taken directly from our love of comics.

For example:

BOOM – The sound made by an explosion, such as, a grenade exploding, a bomb or a missile impact.

CRACK – The sound made by the good team small arms weapons, i.e. pistols, M4s, MP5s etc.

CRACK – (in bold) – The sound made by the good guys sniper rifles.

DAT - The sound made by the enemy's small arms weapons, i.e. pistols, M4s, MP5s etc.

DAT – (in bold) - The sound made by the enemy's sniper rifles.

Italics – Thoughts or radio communications.

THUD – The sound made from blunt force trauma to the body, such as, an elbow, a punch, a kick or a knee. It could also be because of a non-penetrating weapon such as a club, or an axe attack

A definitive glossary can be found at www.10regiment.com.

Chapter 1

Emma blinked rapidly as hundreds of camera flashes erupted in front of her. She turned her head away from the lights and reporters yelling out questions. To her right were the three other winners of the Fortnite Battle Royale competition, though what they had won was still unclear other than it being "the next evolution in Fortnite". To her left were four horizontal pods that were large enough to fit a human inside, but she hoped she wouldn't have to find that out by going inside one.

'Good evening and welcome winners. My name is Josh. Are you ready to experience the next evolution in Fortnite?

'Yes,' replied the four winners.

Josh turned to the reporters and smiled. 'I think they're a bit nervous.' He turned back to the winners. 'Don't worry, it's just us here, oh and 100 million people around the world live streaming this event. Can I please ask you to state your name and age?'

'Emma, I'm 14.'

'Jack, 13.'

'Sophia, 10.'

'Aiden, 11.'

'Today, the world's greatest game, Fortnite, is being merged with 10 Regiment's M.I.S.T. Pods technology. Today is about the future of gaming and you four are going to show it off to the world.'

Emma looked at the other winners, Sophia and Aiden could barely contain their excitement. Jack already looked bored. Emma turned back to Josh as he continued to speak, however now, he was facing the cameras instead of her.

'In just a few minutes, the world's four luckiest gamers are going to climb into the pods and be transported directly into the world of Fortnite where they will enter a solo match for the entire world to see. I'll take a few questions while our winners enter the pods.'

Emma nearly vomited. She'd be going into the pods and showing the world how afraid of she was of small spaces. She turned away from the pods to control her nerves.

'Are you going to faint?' asked Jack, recording her panic attack on his phone.

Emma pushed his phone away from her face.

'Can any of you actually play?' asked Aiden.

'I usually win or finish in the top three,' said Jack.

'Same,' said Emma.

'I like to hide and dance. I got my first kill last week,' said Sophia proudly.

'You're a camper, that's great,' said Jack in a tone that made Sophia stop smiling.

The four winners were moved towards the pods by staff wearing skins from inside the game.

'Wait here, as we power up the pods,' said a person dressed in a red knight skin.

The four winners huddled together. Emma stood with her back to the pods, chanting to herself, please don't vomit, please don't vomit, please don't vomit.

'Should we have a code?' asked Sophia.

'Why?' asked Aiden.

'So, we can help each other.'

'There's no helping each other in solo games, though it hardly matters, I don't think you'll be around for long,' said Jack.

Aiden high-fived him.

'Ten,' said Emma, looking at Sophia.

'I don't understand,' said Sophia.

'If in doubt, say a number under ten, if it's one of us, we'll answer with whatever number adds up to ten. If they say the wrong number or don't reply, it's not one of us, okay.'

'If you ask me to do math when I'm inside the game, I'll head shot you for sure,' said Jack.

'What if you're too far away to hear me?' asked Sophia.

Emma placed a hand on Sophia's trembling shoulder.

'What would you like to do, so we know it is you?'

'I like to dance.'

Jack laughed so loud, the technician behind him almost fell inside the pod they were working on.

'Oh my god, I hope I get to see you get blown away while you're dancing!'

'I still don't get how they let a noob showcase the game to the world,' said Aiden.

'You have my word. If I see you, I will help you,' said Emma.

Chapter 2

Emma climbed into her pod and rolled onto her back. The technician assigned to her pod connected electrodes to either side of her forehead.

'I'm all done. Just relax,' said the technician in a soothing tone.

'I'll relax if you lie to me and tell me the glass top isn't going to be lowered on top of me.'

'Don't worry, a few seconds after the canopy closes, a gas will be pumped into the pod and put you to sleep.'

'How is drugging me to sleep supposed to make me worry less?' whispered Emma. 'One hundred million people are watching me. What if I drool? UH! What if I fart!'

The technician smiled.

'Since the news got out that we're inserting you directly into the game, it's closer to 350 million people watching you and that number is rising rapidly. Good luck.'

The technician stepped back. The pod canopy lowered towards her.

'Just breathe…Come on gas, knock me out. I just want this to be over.'

A cool, gentle breeze from behind her passed over her head. The camera flashes erupted once more as her eyes closed.

***

Emma opened her eyes. She was a default avatar wearing brown pants and a green singlet top standing on a circular grey podium. The three other podiums in the room, two to her left and one to her right were empty. She recognized this room though she'd never seen it from this angle. The room had no doors or windows, just concrete on every surface except for the wall directly in front of her which was made from glass. Standing in this room, she knew the matchmaking process was underway, searching for enough gamers to fill the battle bus. She was seconds away from deploying.

'Hello Emma, my name is Fiona. How are you feeling?'

Emma looked at the woman that had just appeared on the screen of glass in front of her.

'This is so weird!'

'You'll be deploying shortly, though before you do, you need to know that playing Fortnite from inside the game has a few differences from how you normally play at home.'

'Okay,' said Emma.

'When you're in the game, you'll have a display strapped to your non-dominant forearm. You'll be able to configure through several screens such as the map and the inventory. You'll still need to axe resources but when you want to build, select a weapon or switch screens on your display, you only need to think about it and the structure, screen or weapon you want will appear. The most important part of your display is the green health bar and the blue shield bar at the top. This display allows you to see everything you'd normally see when playing. Only you and the other three winners will have a display, so I'm sorry if wearing it makes you a prized target to the other gamers that didn't win the competition. If you die, you'll return to this room and follow the others still inside the game in spectator mode. Lastly, you won't feel pain in the simulator, so try and relax and have fun with it. We've filled the battle bus, so it's time to deploy. Good luck.'

'Thank you.'

Large writing appeared on the screen.

Standby for deployment.

A countdown started on the wall.

5, 4, 3, 2, 1, 0

Emma fell through the podium. She didn't even have time to scream before her feet hit the ground. She quickly turned around in a full circle. She was on respawn island. People were appearing out of nowhere. A battle bus was waiting in the distance. In the space between the avatars and the battle bus was randomly scattered weapons and ammo which people were running towards. She scanned the avatars around her. A woman with a display on her arm was running towards her with an astronaut chasing her, swinging their axe.

'Help me, seven,' yelled Sophia.

Emma held out her arms to her.

'Three, I've got you, it's okay. They can't hurt you here.'

The island disappeared.

Emma was hundreds of feet in the air, sitting alone on a single chair inside a tiny metal cubicle. To her left was a small rectangular window. To her right was a door that opened inwards. On the wall in front of her was a flashing yellow button with the words: Thank the bus driver. She looked down at the display on her arm. Her name, Emma14 was above the full green health bar.

Map

The map appeared as soon as she thought about it. The flight path of the battle bus was visible. It was on a South-West flight path, from Risky Reels to Flush Factory. There was a timer showing how long she had before she could exit the battle bus.

6, 5, 4, 3, 2, 1, 0.

'Oh god, I'm going to have to jump!'

Emma could already hear the doors swing open from other cubicles and the avatars running towards the back of the bus. She stood up, hit the button to thank the bus driver and reached for door handle.

Jack's Solo Game

Chapter 3

Jack was hundreds of feet in the air, sitting alone on a single chair inside a tiny metal cubicle. To his left was a small rectangular window. To his right was a door that opened inwards. On the wall in front of him was a flashing yellow button with the words: Thank the bus driver. He looked down at the display on his arm. His name, Jack13, was above the full green health bar.

Map

The map appeared as soon as he thought about it. The flight path of the battle bus was visible. It was on a South-West flight path, from Risky Reels to Flush Factory. There was a timer showing how long he had before he could exit the battle bus.

6, 5, 4, 3, 2, 1, 0.

Jack decided to wait. Today was all about the win in front of 350 million future subscribers. This game had to be epic. He could already hear the doors swing open from other cubicles and the avatars running towards the back of the bus. The battle bus flew past Tomato Temple, then past Dusty Divot and was approaching Salty Springs as he stood up, hit the button to thank the bus driver and reached for the door handle. He stepped into the empty isle and turned towards the back of the bus. The door was open.

Let's do this!

Jack ran at full speed and launched himself through the air. He angled his body head first in a vertical dive as the air ripped at his clothes and body. Seconds later, he arched his back and turned to the left and continued his free fall descent with the barren landscape of Paradise Palms in front of him. The ground was rushing towards him, he was watching it, mesmerized by it when he remembered the ground wasn't rushing towards him, he was, in fact, falling from the sky like a rock.

Glider

The glider deployed. He looked up and sighed. He hadn't had a default glider since season 1.

Jack drifted into Paradise Palms alone, as far as he could tell. He flew straight at the first tall building. At the last minute, he jagged the glider to the left, just in case someone was tailing him and performed a rapid circling descent into the corner of a fenced pool area towards a gold chest. The chimes got louder as he flew closer. Ten yards, five yards, touch down.

Search

The chest opened, revealing shockwave grenades and a green sub-machine gun with ammo. Not the best gold chest he'd ever encountered. He turned and slashed at the concrete pool wall with his axe. Four strikes and the section crumbled. He ran into the house, slashing at everything within arm's reach and discovered another gold chest.

Search

He ran over the ammo, the steel and the small shield potion and crouched in the corner before taking two gulps of the potion. He ran along the wall, swinging his axe against the wall and bushes, collecting as many resources as he could. He ran over a grey assault rifle and it disappeared into his inventory. He entered the house through another door and ran straight towards the green tactical shotgun and ammo. He paused to check his display. He'd been in the game for two and half minutes, not seen a single person, yet only 59 gamers were left.

Tactical shotgun.

He pumped a shell into the chamber as he ran up the stairs. A blue pump shotgun and ammo tempted him in front of a large glass window on the second floor.

Dump the tactical shotgun.

Pick up Pump shotgun.

Jack ran past a bedroom and stopped when he heard the chimes of a gold chest. He entered the room.

Search

He ran over the ammo and wood.

Dump the grenades and grey assault rifle

Pick up slurp juice and green M16

Pump shotgun

Jack ran to the roof and found another slurp juice. He crouched behind a small brick wall and drank the entire jar. He checked his display. He was just inside the first storm boundary and only 45 gamers remained.

Slurp Juice

M16

Jack ran inside and quickly descended the stairs. This was taking too long. He had to find someone to shoot, anyone, even Sophie, or the viewers will be watching the other three gamers instead of him. He ran to the window on the second story and jumped through it.

Ramp

A brick ramp formed underneath him. He jumped to the ground and ran across the street. Paradise Palms was a ghost town. So far, he hadn't even heard a single shot. Maybe he should've gone to Tilted Towers and rolled the dice.

Axe

He swung at everything he ran past, though now, it was more to vent his frustration than to collect resources. He caught movement in the corner of his field of vision.

M16

Jack turned towards the closest building on the other side of the street.

Ramp

He ran onto the rooftop and slowed to a walk as he stalked his prey. The other gamer showed no sign of Jack's presence.

Jack crouched and raised his M16 to his shoulder.

CRACK, CRACK, CRACK, CRACK.

He missed...every shot. The other game jumped off the back of the building they were on and disappeared.

Jack dropped from the rooftop and sprinted towards the brick wall surrounding the other house.

A golf cart's engine started in the distance.

Ramp

Jack climbed the ramp and jumped over the fence. A lone gamer was escaping in a golf cart down an empty road.

'NO!'

Jack raised his M16 to his shoulder.

CRACK, CRACK – 26.

He hit him. The golf cart continued over a small mound. Jack ran as fast as he could. As he reached the top of the mound. He saw where the gamer was heading. A blue wooden supply drop with a yellow and white balloon above it and blue smoke rising into the sky had just landed to the left of the road just ahead of the golf cart.

The golf cart veered to the right, behind a large boulder. Leaving only the front of it visible.

Jack ran across the open ground, completely exposed.

Ramp, Ramp, Ramp, Walls, thought Jack spinning in a circle.

The other gamer was in survival mode, hiding behind the boulder. Suddenly, the golf cart's engine started and drove forward.

CRACK, CRACK, CRACK, CRACK, CRACK, CRACK, CRACK, CRACK, CRACK, CRACK, CRACK, CRACK.

The golf cart hit a dirt mound and tipped forward in the air. The driver recovered and drove towards the closest ridge.

CRACK, CRACK - 31, CRACK - 30, CRACK - 30, CRACK – 20.

The driver vanished. His loot scattered across the dirt, awaiting any scavenger that passed by.

Jack turned away from his first kill in the game. He jumped down the ramp and ran towards the supply drop.

Search

Dump Pump shotgun

Pick up Gold Heavy shotgun

Jack ran over the brick but left the boogie bomb and shield potion.

Heavy shotgun

Jack looked at his display. He was still inside the storm boundary and only 29 gamers remained. It was time to leave Paradise Palms and go hunting for a Victory Royale. He ran towards the loot of his only kill and more importantly, the golf cart. He ran a quick circle around the ammo but left the pathetic weapons in the dirt where they belonged. He sat inside the golf cart.

Drive

He drove towards the edge of Paradise Palms, heading towards Salty Springs. After only a few seconds, he cleared the gully he was in and approached a collection of old wooden buildings.

Exit

Axe

Jack ran towards the buildings, carving up cactus and stacks of wooden pallets at will. He ran through bundles of ammo scattered around the base of at the building overlooking a rundown metal bridge, spanning the canyon in front of him. He jumped from the building onto the bridge and ran towards the gap that separated the two sides.

Floor, Floor.

Wooden floorboards appeared under his feet as he ran into the void, trusting the software that the floors would appear. He crossed onto the grassy side of the canyon and after a quick scan to confirm he was still alone, proceeded to axe everything in sight.

Map

He looked at his display. He was well outside the next storm boundary with just over one minute before the storm began to close. He looked at how many gamers were left, 20 remained. He sighed at his kill count next to the remaining gamers. He had to move. No-one was going to remember him if he finished the game with only one kill. He need something epic.

M16

He started running and bounding North towards the safety of the next storm boundary.

DAT

A single bullet from a sniper rifle ripped through the air somewhere in front of him. He continued his path, directly towards the sound of the shot.

A trumpet echoed throughout the game.

Map

The storm was shrinking.

Jack approached the Southern edge of Dusty Divot, up ahead, another gamer was bounding forward along the cliff edge, mirroring Jacks movements. The gamer veered off to the right behind higher ground.

Walls thought Jack, spinning in a circle.

DAT, DAT, DAT, DAT, DAT.

The gamer fired from his elevated position down on Jack.

Ramp, Ramp, Ramp, Ramp

One hundred yards in front of Jack, the other gamer was building a ramp of his own, neither gamer turned away from the fight in front of such a larger audience.

Jack ran to the top of his ramp and raised his M16 to his shoulder. The other gamer was already in position in front of him, aiming his weapon straight at him.

DAT, DAT, DAT, DAT

Jack jumped backwards, firing at the same time.

CRACK, CRACK – 30, CRACK – 26, CRACK – 20, CRACK, CRACK

Jack landed on the ground.

'WALLS!' he screamed as he spun around. He looked up. 'Ceiling'.

DAT, DAT, DAT, DAT, DAT, DAT, DAT, DAT, DAT, DAT, DAT, DAT

The bullets slammed into the wooden structure protecting him.

Ceiling

DAT, DAT, DAT, DAT

Ceiling

DAT, DAT, DAT, DAT

Ceiling

The bullets ripped the protective roof away almost as fast as Jack could build it. One of the side walls disappeared. Jack ran forward.

Ceiling, Ceiling, Ceiling

Jack ran under the cover of the ceilings as the gamer above he peppered his structure blindly.

Sub-machine gun

Jack stepped out from cover and ripped the middle of the gamer's ramp apart with bullets.

CRACK, CRACK, CRACK, CRACK, CRACK, CRACK, CRACK, CRACK, CRACK, CRACK, CRACK, CRACK, CRACK, CRACK, CRACK, CRACK, CRACK, CRACK, CRACK, CRACK

The ramp collapsed, and the other gamer wasn't happy about it.

Walls, thought Jack spinning.

DAT, DAT, DAT, DAT, DAT, DAT, DAT, DAT, DAT, DAT, DAT, DAT, DAT, DAT, DAT, DAT, DAT, DAT, DAT, DAT, DAT, DAT, DAT, DAT

Ramp, Ramp

Jack jumped onto the bottom of his ramp just as the other gamer appeared at the top. For the briefest of milliseconds, they stared at each other in mutual respect of a battle well fought…and then the respect was over.

CRACK, CRACK - 18, CRACK - 18, CRACK - 20, CRACK - 18, CRACK - 20, CRACK, CRACK, CRACK, CRACK, CRACK, CRACK, CRACK, CRACK, CRACK

The gamer vanished well before Jack stopped shooting. The gamer was dead, and it was a battle that viewers would remember which is what Jack wanted. Some of them might even subscribe to his You-tube channel.

DAT, DAT, DAT, DAT, DAT, DAT, DAT, DAT, DAT, DAT

'WALLS,' screamed Jack.

He was ambushed, in the middle of his You-tube dream, like the idiot that he was.

'FOCUS!'

Jack spat the words at himself. He looked at his display. His shield was down to a single point. His health was still a solid 100.

Ceiling

Shield potion.

Jack skulled the potion as soon as it appeared in his hand whilst spinning around in circles thinking about walls. Everyone who told him he couldn't multi-task would be eating their words right now. A wall to his right vanished. Jack jumped through the opening, hoping to catch the ambusher off-guard.

It didn't work.

DAT, DAT, DAT, DAT, DAT, DAT, DAT

The gamer jumped at him.

Jack jumped to meet him. No guts, no glory!

Heavy shotgun

CRACK, CRACK

The gamer disappeared. Jack had no idea if it was two perfectly aimed head shots, or if he grazed the gamer who was clinging to life with only a few health points, either way, he didn't care. He'll take the kill, however it occurred.

Walls, Ceiling, thought Jack, determined not to make the same mistake twice.

He crouched in the corner of his make-shift shelter like a naughty boy.

Shield Potion, Slurp Juice

He had one in each hand and drank them like he was at a frat party. He checked his display. His shield was back to 100. Only eleven gamers remained.

Heavy shotgun, Sub-machine-gun, M16

He cycled through his weapons, reloading them before he ventured outside.

Map

The storm edge was almost touching him on the display and he was still outside the next storm boundary.

Door

Jack stepped outside and turned around. The purple wall was coming for him. He heard footsteps above him. He looked up. Someone had built a ramp and was now building floors to get directly above him.

Heavy shotgun

CRACK, CRACK, CRACK, CRACK, CRACK, CRACK, CRACK, CRACK, CRACK, CRACK, CRACK, CRACK, CRACK

The structure crumbled. The gamer fell to ground in front of Jack.

CRACK, CRACK - 35, CRACK – 30, CRACK - 28

BOOM…SWOOSH

The rocket flew past Jack's head. They both ran for the walls and ramps remaining from Jacks last battle. Jack raised his heavy shotgun to his shoulder and rounded the corner of his wooden wall. The gamer's head was directly in front of the shotgun's barrel.

CRACK

The gamer vanished. He'd made the top 10.

Walls and ramp, thought Jack spinning.

Slurp juice

Jack drank and took a moment to breath and question whether anyone else was fighting each other or whether they were all lining up somewhere, waiting to take their turn to kill the guy wearing the display.

Another rocket ripped through the air and Jack figured it was aimed at him. He jumped off the edge of the ramp seconds before the rocket blew the structure apart. He ran to the loot from his last kill and spun in a circle.

Walls

Med kit

He wrapped the bandages on him, surging his health back to 100. It was time to find the person with the endless supply of rockets. He noticed an object at his feet.

Rift-to-go

Jack shook the orb and fell from a fracture in the sky high above his previous location.

Glider

Map

He was right inside the next storm boundary. He looked down. A battle erupted beneath him in middle of Dusty Divot. He turned his glider towards the fight. He was almost at the top of the trees when he saw a woman stepping out of a tiny hut wearing an arm display. He pulled his glider hard to the right. He was determined to take out Emma.

Jack's feet hit the ground less than a hundred yards away from Emma and so far, he had remained undetected. He glanced quickly at his display. Only 5 gamers remaining. He was so close to winning the Victory Royale. So close to cementing his name in the history books in front of over 350 million viewers.

The Floss emote music rippled through the area, causing Jack to look up from his display. Emma was flossing as a person crept up behind her. His heart sank. This wasn't Emma. This was Sophia. He was about to get what he boasted about earlier, he'd get to watch her die whilst dancing.

Sophia looked so happy, standing on the grass near the edge of the cliff, dancing in the sunlight.

Something primal erupted from deep inside Jack.

Ramp, Ramp, Ramp, Ramp

Jack bounded up the ramp

Heavy shotgun

CRACK, CRACK, CRACK, CRACK, CRACK - 30, CRACK - 32, CRACK - 30, CRACK - 28, CRACK, CRACK, CRACK, CRACK, CRACK, CRACK, CRACK, CRACK, CRACK, CRACK, CRACK, CRACK, CRACK, CRACK, CRACK, CRACK - 20, CRACK, CRACK

The gamer behind Sophia disappeared.

Sophia jumped.

'SIX!'

'Emma, 6. Emma, where are you?'

CRACK, CRACK, CRACK, CRACK

Sophia shot her common pistol in every direction except for the direction of Jack or the gamer that had been behind her.

Jack ran straight at her.

'Sophia, four. I've got you!'

DAT, DAT, DAT, DAT, DAT, DAT, DAT, DAT, DAT

Bullets slammed into Jack and the ground around Sophia. He held his arms out, making himself a bigger target to draw the gamer's fire towards him and not her. He was two yards from her. He jumped.

'WALLS! CEILING!'

Slurp juice

Jack started drinking. He glanced at Sophia's display and handed the jar to her, so she could drink the last third.

Sophia looked up at Jack.

'Why are you helping me, Jack?'

'I'm not. Teaming up is illegal in solo mode. It can get a person banned. We just happen to be in the same fort, at the same time. It's time to put your pistol away.'

M16

Jack handed his M16 to Sophia.

'Do you know how to use this?'

Sophia nodded.

'Ramp'

Both Jack and Sophia jumped onto the ramp as it formed. Jack checked his display and then turned his head to face Sophia.

'There are 4 gamers left. That means there's two of them and two of us. Given that I can't hear any gunshots, I can guarantee they have teamed up against us. If I was them, I'd split the direction of attack. I'll take the left side, you take the right side. When I remove the ceiling, have you got my back? Are you ready to get your crazy on?'

Sophia's eyes watered.

'Thanks for this, Jack. I'll never forget this. You're the best.'

'Honestly, that's the worst crazy war face I've ever seen.'

'OKAY ON THREE, WE'RE GOING TO REMOVE THE CEILING AND START SHOOTING,' yelled Jack, shaking his head side to side as he said it which made Sophia smile.

Jack held up one finger. Sophia nodded.

'OKAY ON THREE….ONE!'

Jack removed the ceiling and Sophia joined him on the edge of the ramp sending a barrage of bullets into the surrounding forest.

CRACK, CRACK, CRACK, CRACK, CRACK, DAT, CRACK, CRACK, DAT, DAT, DAT, DAT, CRACK, CRACK, CRACK, DAT, DAT, CRACK, CRACK, CRACK, DAT, DAT, DAT,CRACK, CRACK, CRACK, CRACK, CRACK, CRACK, CRACK, CRACK, CRACK, CRACK, CRACK, CRACK, CRACK, CRACK, CRACK, CRACK, CRACK.

'THE FORT…SHOOT THE FORT!' yelled Jack as he shifted his point of fire to the middle of the fort. He caught a glimpse of one of the gamers inside and focus on him like a laser as he felt the other gamer's bullets slam into his back.

CRACK, CRACK, CRACK - 30, DAT, DAT, DAT, CRACK, CRACK - 30, CRACK, CRACK -30, CRACK - 30, CRACK - 30, CRACK, CRACK, DAT, DAT

The gamer in the fort disappeared as Jack swung his weapon around to find the other gamer.

CRACK - 30, DAT, DAT, DAT, CRACK, CRACK - 30, CRACK, CRACK -30

Jack startled as he stood inside the spectator's room. Emma ran forward and hugged him.

'Look at what you did!' said Emma, facing him towards the glass screen at the front of the room.

Sophia stood on the ramp, M16 by her side, surrounded by Jack's loot with a banner hovering above her, #1 Victory Royal.

'Go on Sophia…you know what to do,' urged Jack.

Sophia knew exactly what to do.

She jumped down from the ramp and found a patch of sun and danced the best floss she had ever danced with over half a billion-people cheering her on.

Emma's Solo Game

Chapter 4

Emma was hundreds of feet in the air, sitting alone on a single chair inside a tiny metal cubicle. To her left was a small rectangular window. To her right was a door that opened inwards. On the wall in front of her was a flashing yellow button with the words: Thank the bus driver. She looked down at the display on her arm. Her name, Emma14 was above the full green health bar.

Map

The map appeared as soon as she thought about it. The flight path of the battle bus was visible. It was on a South-West flight path, from Risky Reels to Flush Factory. There was a timer showing how long she had before she could exit the battle bus.

6, 5, 4, 3, 2, 1, 0.

'Oh god, I'm going to have to jump!'

Emma could already hear the doors swing open from other cubicles and the avatars running towards the back of the bus. She stood up, hit the button to thank the bus driver and reached for the door handle. She pulled the door open and stepped into the aisle. Another gamer with an arm display was standing in front of the cubicle on the other side of the aisle wearing a default skin.

'Can you believe we have to wear these skins?' said Emma.

The gamer shrugged. 'People will remember me for my kills, not my looks.'

'Are you Jack or Aiden?'

'Aiden. I'm guessing you're Emma?'

'Yep, so where are you dropping into?'

'Why don't you tell me where you're dropping into first?'

Emma smiled. Neither of them was stupid. She glanced at her display and sprinted down the aisle. On her last step, she launched herself out of the bus, straight into a head-first dive. Loot lake and Tilted Towers was straight in front of her. Something tapped her left foot. She looked back. Aiden was free-falling less than one yard away from her. She flew past the floating island hovering above loot lake. She was sure Aiden would try and kill her the moment they landed together. She changed her mind about her drop point.

Glider

The glider handles appeared in her hands. She pulled the glider hard to her right, catching Aiden off-guard as he continued racing towards Tilted Towers. Her new destination was the floating island which was always an intense place to drop into. She counted at least ten gamers around her flying to the same location.

Emma drifted past the lower outer section of the island. She just cleared the trees guarding the roof of the house. She was coming in fast. There was too much at stake for a soft landing today. She was over the extension at the front of the house. She was lined up to hit the main section of the roof, right in the middle between the two apexes. She bent her knees and braced for the impact.

THUD

She swung her arms back and was halfway through her first swing when the axe appeared in her hand. The head of the axe smashed into the roof as another gamer landed only a few yards away from her. Emma had to get through the first. Two strikes later, the roof crumbled beneath her feet as gunshots erupted from the ground below. She dropped to the floor below. A gold chest was directly in front of her.

Search

THUD!

The other gamer fell through the roof behind her.

Emma picked up the Burst Assault rifle and grenades and spun on her heels. She raised her assault rifle to her shoulder. The other gamer fled the room by jumping out of the roof, down to the ground below. Emma stood on the edge of the roof, scanning for her target, but they were hiding in the foliage of a large tree.

DAT, DAT, DAT, DAT, DAT, DAT.

Bullets from another gamer flew past her head.

She stepped off the roof and dropped to the ground. She quickly scanned her immediate area left to right. The gamer from the roof was crouching at the base of the house armed only with their axe. The gamer looked down in submission, away from the barrel of Emma's assault rifle.

CRACK – 58, CRACK – 29, CRACK – 28.

The gamer vanished leaving behind only a pile of wood that they collected from the roof. Emma scooped up the wood and turned around. Today, with so many people watching her, no mercy would be given, nor asked for. This was her chance to build a global reputation.

Emma ran past the tree that had concealed the gamer seconds earlier and jumped off a small cliff to the dirt section below her without any regard or caution for her own safety. A gamer ran under her as she dropped through the air.

CRACK.

She missed the shot. She followed the other gamer's movement with her assault rifle as they jumped and turned in mid-air.

CRACK – 28, CRACK – 28, CRACK – 29, CRACK.

The gamer turned and ran towards an underground mine shaft as soon as their feet hit the dirt.

Emma chased them relentlessly. She jumped towards him and opened fire through the air.

CRACK – 29, CRACK, CRACK – 58.

The last shot was almost point blank. The gamer disappeared. Emma grabbed their assault rifle as it fell to the ground and continued running towards the mine shaft. She had to find a shield potion as a priority. She made it to the entrance of the mine shaft as a gamer landed on the dirt next to a large boulder, twenty yards to her left. She opened fire on full-auto.

CRACK – 31, CRACK – 31, CRACK – 31, CRACK – 31, CRACK – 31.

Emma kept her sights on the gamer until she was sure they had disappeared and then turned back to the mine shaft and ran inside.

Axe

She swung at the rocks and wooden boxes positioned on the side of the floorboards as she ran deeper into the mine shaft. Suddenly, she heard footsteps to her right.

Assault rifle

Emma turned to her right firing first from her hip and then aimed shots from her shoulder as the other gamer ran around the corner into her spray of bullets.

CRACK, CRACK, CRACK, CRACK – 29, CRACK.

Only one bullet hit its mark as the other gamer bounced to the right like her life depended on it, because it did. Emma followed her movement with her assault rifle and waited for her to land in the spot she had predicted.

DAT, DAT, DAT – 30.

Emma got hit in her arm.

Wall

Emma sealed the mine shaft between her and the other gamer with a wooden wall as the gamer continued to fire from the other side.

The wall disappeared under the barrage of bullets. Emma jumped forward, past the gamer and spun in the air to face her. The other gamer jumped and turned but it was too late.

CRACK – 31

The gamer vanished in mid-air.

DAT, DAT.

Emma shunted forward. She turned her body after being hit in the back, weapon raised with eyes as wide as dinner plates. The mine shaft was being over-run by gamers.

CRACK – 62, CRACK – 31.

The other gamer opened fire.

DAT, DAT, DAT, DAT.

Emma dodged to the left just in time. She returned fire.

CRACK, CRACK, CRACK, CRACK, CRACK – 61.

The last bullet did the job. The gamer disappeared. She ran through the items the gamer left behind, scooping up wood, a rare pistol, ammo and another assault rifle, but still no shield. She looked down at her display, six kills in the first minute…not bad, but she only had twenty-four health points remaining. She couldn't continue this kind of fighting without a shield or a med kit. She ran out of the mine shaft, ignoring the gamers in the distance locked in a fight to the death and launched herself off the southern edge of the floating island. She fell for less than a second when an idea flashed into her head.

Glider

Emma flew back up to the lower section of the island as the glider filled with the updraft from below. She flew around half of the island, searching for either a med-kit, bandages or a shield potion from the eliminated gamers. There was nothing, but dirt.

Free-fall

Emma fell through the air, on a rapid descent to Loot Lake where gamers were scurrying around in fierce gun battles in the knee-deep water below her. She steered her glider to a boulder at the top of the first waterfall in the center of Loot Lake. Her legs hit the water that was so cold it took her breath away. Until now, she'd never even thought of the temperature of the water that she would send her avatars into without hesitation. On the other side of the boulder were two gamers going head-to-head. As far as Emma could tell, neither had noticed her arrival.

Assault rifle

Despite only having twenty-four health points, Emma entered the fight.

CRACK – 70, CRACK, CRACK, CRACK – 31.

One down, one to go.

The surviving gamer jumped high into the air. Emma followed them through her sights.

CRACK, CRACK – 31, CRACK – 31, CRACK – 62.

They disappeared.

Emma ran towards the loot left behind by the pair. Bobbing around in the water was a jug of slurp juice and a grappler among an armory of rifles and ammo. She crouched in the water and gulped down the slurp juice without any protection, figuring that putting up walls would only make her position more obvious to the other gamers in the area. Her health points instantly began to increase.

Emma waited just a couple of seconds until her health points had climbed over seventy. She turned and jumped over the first waterfall and bounded towards the center of the vortex to use the strong updraft to push her into the air, so she could scout out the area properly. She crouched in the water, one jump away from the vortex, to conduct a final scan of the area. It was as safe as it was going to get. She jumped into the vortex and was pushed into the air. She instantly saw two things, there was another slurp juice available in the water, and there was a gamer sheltering behind a rock that she could have only seen from above them.

Emma turned her body out of the wind. She aimed for a boulder that towered over the rock the gamer was hiding behind. She needed to get there fast. She waited until the last possible second to slow down.

Glider

The glider deployed in her hand slowing her down just enough to not lose health points when she collided into the boulder.

Assault rifle

She crept up the boulder, assault rifle in hand and peered over the edge.

CRACK – 31, CRACK – 31

The gamer threw a grenade. It hit the edge of the rock they were hiding behind and disappeared into the water between their feet.

BOOM

The gamer was gone.

Emma rushed forward and picked up the slurp juice.

Ramp

Emma climbed out of the water and couched on the third step of the ramp. She drank the slurp juice.

DAT, DAT, DAT.

The glass jar exploded in front of Emma's face. She jumped off the ramp, looking where the shots had come from as she flew.

Assault rifle

CRACK – 85, DAT, DAT, CRACK -17.

They disappeared.

Emma ran through the loot, collecting the ammo, but not stopping for anything else. She climbed her ramp once more and paused at the top, scanning for targets.

DAT

Emma looked around the room she was standing in. There were four active windows on the screen in front of her. Her match stats were displayed in one of the windows: Emma14, nine kills, match time – One minute and fifty-six seconds. A replay of her elimination showed a gamer with a gold sniper rifle used the vortex to drop in behind her. She was taken out by a head shot at close range. She looked at the other windows. Jack was in Paradise Palms and yet to get a single kill. Aiden had already eliminated five other gamers in Tilted Towers and was looking good. Emma turned her head to Sophia's window and smiled. Sophia was hard core camping inside a hut, armed only with a pistol and had zero eliminations.

Emma sighed. It stung a little for her to be the first to be eliminated, but going by the statistics of the other winners, she was easily the gamer that had gone out with the most aggression and she was hoping that will lead to a bump in subscribers on her You-Tube channel.

Aiden's Solo Game

Chapter 5

Aiden was hundreds of feet in the air, sitting alone on a single chair inside a tiny metal cubicle. To his right was a small rectangular window. To his left was a door that opened inwards. On the wall in front of him was a flashing yellow button with the words: Thank the bus driver. He looked down at the display on his arm. His name, Aiden11 was above the full green health bar.

Map

The map appeared as soon as he thought about it. The flight path of the battle bus was visible. It was on a South-West flight path, from Risky Reels to Flush Factory. There was a timer showing how long he had before he could exit the battle bus. He stood up, hit the button to thank the bus driver and waited for the countdown to reach zero which would unlock the back door of the battle bus.

6, 5, 4, 3, 2, 1, 0.

Aiden opened the door and stepped into the aisle. From the moment he was told he was one of the competition winners, he knew his target would be Tilted Towers, regardless of the Battle bus's flight path for his match.

A door opened in front of him on the other side of the aisle. Another gamer with an arm display stepped into the aisle wearing a default skin.

'Can you believe we have to wear these skins?' said Emma.

Aiden shrugged. 'People will remember me for my kills, not my looks.'

'Are you Jack or Aiden?'

'Aiden. I'm guessing you're Emma?'

'Yep, so where are you dropping into?'

'Why don't you tell me where you're dropping into first?'

Emma smiled.

Aiden smiled back at her.

Emma looked down at her display. She sprinted down the aisle and disappeared out of the bus.

She took him by surprise.

Aiden chased after her. He caught up to her during the free-fall. He reached out and tapped her foot with his hand, so she knew he was there. Their formation was so tight, they looked like fighter jets as they flew towards Loot lake and Tilted Towers.

Emma's glider suddenly ripped her out of the formation. She was full of surprises.

Aiden resisted the temptation to follow her. Today was too important to be distracted. He would stick to his plan. He continued his descent towards Tilted Towers.

Glider

Aiden flew straight towards the first tall building from Loot Lake with a gold chest on the roof. He lined it up in a way so he didn't have to flare or weave the glider to shave off speed or altitude. He lifted his legs to his chest, just managing to clear the concrete wall that wrapped around the outside of the roof. He landed between the two metal air-conditioning ducts and ran towards the gold chest.

Search

A gamer landed behind Aiden and tried to push him out of the way as he was picking up an M16. He turned and unleashed a swarm of bullets in the gamer's direction.

CRACK, CRACK, CRACK, CRACK, CRACK -19, CRACK -20, CRACK, CRACK, CRACK.

The gamer jumped into the air and over the side of the building.

Aiden jumped onto the concrete wall and looked down. The impact on the street below killed the gamer. Aiden felt cheated, not quite believing the gamer had robbed him from getting his first kill of the game. He ran along the wall of the roof top and dropped down to the level below. There was nothing useful on the deck outside. He turned and ran through open glass doors into the building. Ahead of him was a corridor with a white wall to his right and two open archways on his left.

A gamer ran through the second archway, exactly where Aiden was looking and was holding his M16.

CRACK, CRACK – 30.

The gamer turned left, running into the closet room, which was directly in front of Aiden.

Aiden opened fire.

CRACK – 30, CRACK – 31, CRACK – 29.

Three bullets hit the gamer's back. His disappeared, leaving his loot on the floor.

Aiden ran forward. He could hear footsteps outside. He collected a shield potion and some ammo and ran back out of the room. He bounded up the stairs and turned into the first room he came across. He picked up the ammo shells and a pump shotgun. He could hear a nearby gold chest, but so far, he couldn't see it.

Axe

Aiden started swinging, tearing the bedroom to pieces and building up his resources in the process. He ran to the other end of the hallway, along brown wooden floorboards that were painfully loud when his foot hit them, giving his location away to anyone within earshot. The sound of the gold box was getting louder. He was going in the right direction. He entered the bedroom. The gold chest was on top of the bed.

Search

He picked up an assault rifle, a small shield potion and some more ammo.

Shield potion

He knelt in the corner and took two drinks of his small potion. He was in good shape.

DAT, DAT!

Someone shot him twice from an unknown location. He ran out of the room and jumped over the handrail of the staircase to the floor below.

Pump shotgun

Aiden spun around. A gamer was standing at the top of the handrail.

CRACK

Aiden shot the gamer from close range. The gamer retreated and jumped out of the building and died on the street from the fall.

'What is happening?'

Aiden's kill count should have read three but was currently stuck on one.

A gamer ran out from behind an old blue car to collect the shotgun from the gamer who had just disappeared.

Aiden lined them up.

CRACK, CRACK – 31.

Aiden jumped. He landed right in front of the gamer who was standing next to the shotgun.

CRACK – 31.

The gamer disappeared leaving some great items behind.

Aiden swooped in and collected the jar of slurp juice, some wood, some stone and remote explosives. He ran back inside the building and drank his large shield potion.

Assault rifle

Two gamers were fighting in the street outside. He ran outside and bounded towards them, he arrived just as the victor of the battle was picking up the items from the fallen gamer. He aimed his rifle at the back of the gamer's head.

CRACK – 31, CRACK – 30, CRACK - 30

Aiden picked up the metal, wood and another small shield potion. He looked up. A gamer entered a building that was still being constructed on the other side a small grassed square in front of him. He stood up and ran towards the building.

Remote explosives

Aiden jumped into the air to get extra distance and threw the explosives as hard as he could. It bounced once before he detonated them.

BOOM

Smoke filled the first floor of the building.

Assault Rifle

Aiden raised his assault rifle to his shoulder and fired as the smoke began to clear.

CRACK, CRACK, CRACK - 32, CRACK, CRACK

The gamer tried to avoid the bullets by jumping but Aiden followed him through the air with his sights.

CRACK, CRACK – 28

Both the smoke and the gamer were gone.

Aiden ran through the loot. Picking up ammo and resources as he went. Someone was running around on the floor above.

Dump remote explosives

Pick up pump shotgun

Assault Rifle

Aiden ran outside into the open. Almost daring the other gamers to engage him. He turned back to the building and lined himself up with the window on the second level. He ran towards the building and jumped into the air.

RAMP

He bounded to the top of the ramp.

DAT, DAT, DAT, DAT, DAT, DAT, DAT, DAT, DAT

A spray of bullets flew out of the window. Only a few hit his body. He turned on the spot.

WALLS, RAMP!

Aiden ascended to the next level and peered over the top of his ramp. The was a camper sitting on top of the next building. He raised his assault rifle to his shoulder.

CRACK – 70, CRACK – 70, CRACK – 40

Aiden checked his display. He was on track, five kills in just under two minutes. He reloaded his assault rifle and jumped from the ramp back onto an outside ledge of the building. He ran around the outside of the third level of the building, past an air-conditioning vent and found and open entry way back inside. Like the rest of the building, the level had a lot of open spaces. Immediately to his left was a drop to the level below and an internal stairwell leading up to the level he was on.

The gamer from the second level ran along the space below Aiden and ran up the stairs.

Pump shotgun

Aiden dropped down behind him and opened fire.

CRACK, CRACK – 70, CRACK

The gamer jumped from the stairs onto the third level floor and built a wall behind him.

'ARRRRGGGHHHH!'

Aiden screamed in frustration.

CRACK, CRACK

He pumped two shots into the wall. The wall crumbled. Another wall appeared.

The other gamer opened fire.

DAT, DAT, DAT, DAT, DAT, DAT, DAT, DAT, DAT

Aiden jumped backwards and created his own wall while still in the air. He fell out of an open window and down to a ledge below.

RAMP

He climbed the ramp to get back into the fight.

DAT, DAT, DAT, DAT, DAT, DAT

Bullets slammed into the wall and ramp around him from behind.

Aiden dropped off the ramp and ran around the edge of the building right into a newly built steel wall. He cautiously rounded the steel wall with his pump shotgun raised to his shoulder. A gamer was crouched right in front of him.

CRACK – 110, CRACK – 85

The gamer was eliminated.

WALLS

Aiden turned, enclosing himself within his own room against the building.

Slurp juice

He drank the entire jug.

Axe

Aiden broke the wall closest to him and ran into the nearest building, swinging wildly at the tables and chairs positioned near the big glass windows.

DAT

A sniper's bullet fired.

Aiden wasn't hit, but it sounded close enough to be more careful. He broke through the window and was immediately fired upon from behind.

WALLS!

A wooden wall separated Aiden and the other gamer. The gamer built two ramps over Aiden's wall and ran up the ramp. Aiden followed the sound of the footsteps along the ramp and waited underneath for the gamer to expose themselves.

The gamer jumped off the end of the ramp.

CRACK – 30

The gamer landed on the street.

DAT, DAT, CRACK – 31, DAT, CRACK – 31

The gamer vanished.

Aiden checked his display, half of his shield was gone, he had seven kills and there were still forty-one gamers remaining in the match. He ran through the ammo and resources of the eliminated gamer and kept moving. He ran away from the building he'd been focused on for most of the game. He bounded past a construction barrier and a yellow school bus. In front of him was a tall brick building with an external staircase.

RAMP, RAMP

He ran up the ramps and jumped for the roof but fell short and landed on a deck with an open archway in front of him.

DAT, DAT, DAT

Bullets flew at Aiden. At least one connected. He stumbled back half a step. He turned to the left and sprinted up the staircase to flee the gamer who had shot him, but he was yet to see. He reached the landing and turned to go up the next flight of stairs when the barrel of his pump shotgun hit the chest of a gamer running down the stairs. The gamer's mouth opened wide. His eyes doubled in size. Aiden pulled the trigger quickly.

CRACK- 86, CRACK – 70

The gamer was gone.

Bullets chased Aiden up the stairs. He continued to the top of the stairs, turned, crouched and waited for the other gamer to follow him. Nothing happened. There was a grey metal door in front of him. He had no idea what was waiting for him on the other side. He looked at his display. His shield was low.

Small potion

He drank from it twice. He decided to risk going through the door. He stood up and opened the door. It led outside onto the roof. He ran along the edge of the roof, searching for targets on the street below. It was empty. He looked up. He was running towards a wall.

RAMP

He climbed the ramp and continued along the new rooftop, searching for targets on the ground. He jumped over an air-conditioning duct and crouched next to a satellite dish on the corner of the roof. From there he spotted elimination number nine crouching behind a brick wall near the cliffs.

Aiden stepped off the roof.

RAMP

The ramp appeared under his feet.

THUD

The other gamer looked up from the brick wall to see what the sound was.

Aiden ran up the ramp and jumped off the edge, twisting his body through the air as he flew over the fence and the gamer.

CRACK – 70

One shot was all it took. Aiden ran through his loot and heard a ripping sound approaching him.

'Oh no.'

He jumped into the air and turned just in time to see the smoke trail from a rocket, it was aimed at the exact point he was about to land.

BOOM

'That had to hurt,' said Emma.

Aiden looked at her and then in the room they were both standing in.

'Please don't say Sophia outlasted me?'

'I'm afraid so,' said Emma.

Aiden looked at the stats in his window on the screen. He nodded.

'Not a bad day's work, nine kills in three minutes and thirty-four seconds. How did you go?'

'See for yourself,' said Emma, pointing at her window.

'Oh, come on, you can't be serious. Nine kills in one minute and fifty-six seconds!'

'I know you said it's not the victory that counts, it's the amount of kills you get. So, does that mean if we got the same number of kills but I did it in half the time that makes me the winner?'

'Maybe. So, tell me, has Sophia moved at all?'

'Not a single step,' said Emma.

'Poor girl. She has no clue how savage the viewers are going to be to her when she gets back into the real world. I wouldn't have even turned up today if I was her.'

'I like that she came,' said Emma.

Sophia's Solo Game

Chapter 6

Sophia was hundreds of feet in the air, sitting alone on a single chair inside a tiny metal cubicle. To her left was a small rectangular window. To her right was a door that opened inwards. On the wall in front of her was a flashing yellow button with the words: Thank the bus driver. She looked down at the display on her arm. Her name, Sophia10 was above the full green health bar.

Map

The map appeared as soon as she thought about it. The flight path of the battle bus was visible. It was on a South-West flight path, from Risky Reels to Flush Factory. There was a timer showing how long she had before she could exit the battle bus.

6, 5, 4, 3, 2, 1, 0.

Her stomach twisted in a knot, which doubled in size when she looked through the window at the ground far below. Sophia could already hear the doors swing open from other cubicles and the gamers running towards the back of the bus.

The battle bus flew over Tomato Temple. Sophia stood up and reached for the door handle with shaking hands. She grasped it on her second attempt and pulled the door towards her. She entered the isle and turned towards the back of the bus.

'Oh, I didn't thank the bus driver!'

Sophia turned back to the door to her cubicle. There was no door handle on this side. She pushed the metal door, but it wouldn't move. It was locked.

'I'm sure everyone is watching the others, but if anyone is watching me, I'm not rude, I'm just scared. I'm sorry I forgot to thank the bus driver.'

Sophia sighed. She's never started a game without thanking the bus driver. She hoped this wasn't a bad omen that she was going to embarrass herself in front of the world.

She walked down the aisle. Every step she took towards the back door was shorter than the step before. By the time she reached the back of the bus, her feet were barely moving forward. She wrapped her fingers around either side of the door frame and leaned into the open void. The passing air did it's best to pull her from the bus.

THUD

'Argh!'

Someone bumped Sophia as they jumped out of the bus. She held onto the door frame with her right hand, but her fingers were slipping.

She closed her eyes, let go and tumbled through the air.

Glider

The glider handles appeared in her hand. Her chest was heaving. Her breaths were so rapid that she couldn't tell if her body was trying to breath in, or out or both at the same time. She did her best to control her breathing, or at least appear like she knew how to breath. She was already bullied at school and online for almost everything she did, said or wore. She didn't need to add breathing to the list of things that everyone thought she was bad at.

She looked down and for the first time, appreciated how beautiful the island was below her. She pulled the glider handles left and right and weaved her way through the air. For the first time in a long time, she found a reason to smile. She looked at the display on her left forearm as other gamers raced past her towards the ground. In front of her was Lonely Lodge, but she didn't think she'd make it all the way. To her right was Retail Row. As a rule, she usually avoided built up areas, but as Jack had said to her before they climbed inside the pods, she was likely to be the first to die, so why not try something new. The buildings were getting closer. Five gamers swooped passed her towards the town.

Sophia lost her courage.

'NOPE!'

She pulled hard on the right handle of her glider. Her descent accelerated. She tried to control the glider, but it was too late. She was going to land, or more specifically, she was going to crash land near the edge of Dusty Divot.

Sophia's feet hit the grass. An axe appeared in her hand. She was out in the open. There was a small mountain to her right. She sprinted towards a small wooden hut that was thirty yards away. She ran up to the window and looked inside. It was clear. She ran to the front of the hut and entered through the open doorway. She scanned the hut. The back wall had one small shelf with bottles on it. There was a wooden box to the right near the door. A single common pistol was on top of a green sleeping bag. There was nothing else inside the hut other than a few scattered books on the floor and a window on the walls to her left and right.

Pick up pistol

Sophia established her camping spot. She crouched behind the wooden box and raised her pistol at the door.

Any second now...

Thirty seconds later, Sophia lowered her pistol. She checked her display. The game had only just started and twenty-five gamers had already been eliminated. She looked at the elimination information. Emma and Aiden were in a frenzy.

They must have gone to Tilted Towers.

Sophia had watched other gamers enter Titled Towers after they'd killed her. She'd even watched her favorite gamers like Loeya and Ninja on Twitch TV eliminate dozens of gamers in a single game. She'd seen enough to know the place wasn't built for her.

Sophia could hear footsteps. They were getting louder. She held her breath. Someone was running towards the hut. She raised her pistol higher and aimed it at the middle of the door. The footsteps were so loud. She saw the gamer.

CRACK!

She missed.

The gamer ran past the hut. They didn't even take the time to stop and put her out of her misery.

I'm so pathetic!

Sophia gave up guarding the door. For the next ten minutes, she watched her display. She hadn't seen Emma or Aiden eliminate anyone in a while. Truth be told, she probably missed it, just like she missed the gamer that ran past her earlier. Jack, on the other hand was a different story. He had more eliminations than her entire family had achieved in the seven months since they first downloaded Fortnite.

Every time the storm closed in, she expected to be outside the circle, but she never was. The hut was her perfectly positioned haven. She checked her display and squealed. She was in the top ten! She started pacing back and forth in excitement along the back wall of the hut. She remembered the live stream viewers were watching her. No doubt, bored out of their brains. As her brother always said, "Nobody likes a camper!". She looked up for no other reason than that's where she thought the invisible camera angle would look the best.

'I just want to say that I'm really sorry to everyone watching. I know anyone else would've done better than me if they won the competition instead of me. I'm not usually like this. I'm mean, if I'm being honest, I'm a camper, not a fighter, that's for sure, but I play Fortnite because I get to be me around one hundred other humans and I don't get bullied, or pushed, or laughed at. Granted, yes, I do get shot, but the way I see it is that I get to explore the island, dressed in skins, dancing and collecting things that other people might need when they kill me.'

Sophia could feel a spark of courage ignite inside her. She stood up and walked closer to the door.

'I have never camped for an entire game and I'm not about to start. So, in front of you all, I pledge that if I make it into the top five, I am going to leave this hut and dance. I'm not a good fighter, I'm not brave and I can't build, but I am here representing all the noobs and campers out there watching today and I am going to do what I do best, I'm going to dance and have fun!'

Sophia jumped and retreated one step back from the doorway as gunshots echoed up from Dusty Divot. She watched her display, bouncing up and down and rocking side to side. The eliminations continued.

Eight gamers left.

Seven gamers left.

Six gamers left.

She was in the top five.

'I get told I'm mental by people at school every day, but this truly is mental. I cannot believe I'm about to do this. World, if you're watching this, prepare to witness something epic!'

Sophia looked down. She was standing just inside the shadow of the hut. In front of her, only one step away was sunlight.

'It's time for me to step into the light!'

Sophia strode confidently through the door. Her body, suddenly bathed in sunlight, soaked up the warmth. In the back of her mind, she hoped her mental act would inspire just one person to live in a way that made them happy. She walked towards the cliffs of Dusty Divot.

Let's start flossing!

The floss emote music rippled through the area drowning out the sounds of battle and looting. She closed her eyes and smiled so wide she thought she might break her face as she basked in her own awesomeness.

A man's voice yelled over the top of her music.

'Ramp, Ramp, Ramp, Ramp'

She opened her eyes. A huge ramp towered in front of her. Someone was jumping up the ramp.

This is it.

CRACK, CRACK

Sophia looked at her display. Not only was she still alive, but she hadn't even been hit. This person was just as bad at shooting as she was.

Pistol!

She remembered Emma's code and hoped she was still alive.

'SIX!'

'Emma, six. Emma, where are you?'

She raised her pistol and yanked the trigger.

CRACK, CRACK, CRACK, CRACK

Aiming was irrelevant. She just wanted to look hard core to the viewers.

The man ran straight at her.

'Sophia, four. I've got you!'

Sophia nearly died of shock. The man knew her name and used the code! He was wearing an arm display.

DAT, DAT, DAT, DAT, DAT, DAT, DAT, DAT, DAT

Something hit her in her back.

The man jumped at her.

'WALLS! CEILING!' he screamed.

Sophia stood silently next to the man. She was safe, inside his building which he constructed faster than Sophia could blink. He started drinking a slurp juice. He looked at Sophia's display and handed the jar to her. She took it and drank the last third. Her mind was racing. So much was happening. Usually she just collected stuff for other people. Now she had been shot, but she was still alive, she was drinking slurp juice and she was pretty sure she was feeling something romantic between her and the man that saved her life.

Sophia looked up at him. It had to be Jack. She had a 50% percent chance it was either Jack or Aiden. She took a gamble.

'Why are you helping me, Jack?'

'I'm not. Teaming up is illegal in solo mode. It can get a person banned. We just happen to be in the same fort, at the same time. It's time to put your pistol away.'

An M16 appeared in Jack's hand. He handed it to her.

Dump pistol

Sophia took the M16.

'Do you know how to use this?' he asked.

Sophia nodded.

'Ramp' said Jack.

Sophia jumped onto the ramp as it formed, just like Jack did. Jack checked his display and then turned to face her.

'There are four gamers left. That means there's two of them and two of us. Given that I can't hear any gunshots, I'm sure they have teamed up against us. If I was them, I'd split the direction of attack. I'll take the left side, you take the right side. When I remove the ceiling, have you got my back? Are you ready to get your crazy on?'

Sophia's eyes watered. This was the first time someone had used the word crazy around her and meant it as a good thing rather than an insult. She took a deep breath. What he's done for her, in front of so many people, his simple act of kindness has given her hope.

'Thanks for this, Jack. I'll never forget this. You're the best.'

'Honestly, that's the worst crazy war face I've ever seen.'

Jack gripped his shotgun tightly.

Attacking people was completely new to Sophia, but Jack looked like he knew what he was doing. She tightened her grip on her M16 for no other reason than she wanted to copy Jack.

'OKAY ON THREE, WE'RE GOING TO REMOVE THE CEILING AND START SHOOTING,' yelled Jack, shaking his side to side as he said it.

Sophia smiled. He was such an idiot.

Jack held up one finger.

Sophia understood. She nodded. They were jumping to certain death on one.

'OKAY ON THREE....ONE!'

Jack removed the ceiling.

Sophia raised her M16 to her shoulder. She stood on the edge of the ramp and pulled the trigger as she searched for targets.

CRACK, CRACK, CRACK, CRACK, CRACK, DAT, CRACK, CRACK, DAT, DAT, DAT, DAT, CRACK, CRACK, CRACK, DAT, DAT, CRACK, CRACK, CRACK, DAT, DAT, DAT, CRACK, CRACK, CRACK, CRACK, CRACK, CRACK, CRACK, CRACK, CRACK, CRACK, CRACK, CRACK, CRACK, CRACK, CRACK, CRACK, CRACK.

Sophia saw a person in front of her. For the first time in her life, she focused on the sights with the intent of eliminating another person. She released the trigger to try to aim better.

'THE FORT...SHOOT THE FORT!' yelled Jack.

Sophia ignored him. There was a gamer standing on their own ramp in front of her that was now in the middle of her sights. She squeezed the trigger.

CRACK, CRACK, CRACK - 30,

OMG, I hit him!

DAT, DAT, DAT, CRACK, CRACK, CRACK, CRACK, CRACK, CRACK, CRACK, CRACK, DAT, DAT

Sophia felt two thuds slam into her. One into her shoulder. The other into her chest, but she wasn't in pain.

Jack swung around to face her direction. They were shoulder to shoulder.

CRACK - 30, DAT, DAT, DAT, CRACK, CRACK - 30, CRACK, CRACK -30

The gamer in front of Sophia disappeared. She was in shock. She turned to Jack, but he was gone. In his place was a treasure trove of weapons and items. She stood alone on the ramp, unsure of what was happening. She checked her display. There was only one person remaining in the game.

The realization of what that meant almost made her fall off the ramp. A sign flashed above her.

#1 Victory Royale

Sophia knew exactly what she had to do. She jumped down from the ramp and found a patch of grass in the sun.

To my hero, Jack, and to all the noobs out there, this one's for you!

Let's start flossing!

Sophia danced the best floss she had ever danced with over half a billion-people cheering her on.

Emma, Aiden, Sophia and Jack

Return from the Pods

Chapter 7

Emma opened her eyes. She was laying in the pod. The glass canopy was raised all the way. For a second, she laid perfectly still, recounting what she'd just experienced inside Fortnite. It was so exhilarating that she wasn't sure she wanted to go back to her normal life now that it was over.

'Welcome back,' said Josh as he stood by the door. 'We've set up a press conference in the next room in ten minutes, so you can tell the world what it was like to be inside the world of Fortnite. While I warm-up them up, I suggest you look at your Twitch and You-tube accounts on your phones.'

Emma sat up. She swung her legs over the side of the pod and stood up. Her phone was in a locker she'd been given in the Epic Headquarters change room. She stood up and walked through the door and down the hallway as Jack, Aiden and Sophia began to show signs of life in their pods.

Emma picked up her phone and unlocked it. The first thing she noticed, she had over one thousand messages. She opened her You-Tube account and dropped the phone. The screen shattered. Emma picked up her phone from the white tiled floor and held it in both hands to try and steady it enough to read the screen. She had eight million You-Tube subscribers. She checked Twitch. She had five million subscribers. That was the same amount as Ninja. She ran out of the locker room.

'Check your phones! You're not going to believe this!'

The other three gamers ran into the locker room. All their subscriber numbers were in the millions, even Sophia's. They were going to be able to play and stream Fortnite like the players they watched before today.

'Check it out,' said Jack, holding up his phone.

Emma looked at what he was showing her. It was a list of the most popular trending hashtags on the internet. She read them out loud.

'#FortnitePods, #MyHeroJack, #LethalEmma, #AidentheAssassin and #Imacampertoo.'

'What?' asked Sophia. 'I've got a hashtag too?'

'You've not only got the hashtag, but you got the Victory Royale. You're a superstar.'

'She's also got sponsorship offers from actual camping companies,' said Fiona, the technician that had talked to the gamers whilst they were inside the game. 'You've all got different offers coming in. I'm not sure you realize yet, but you're lives have changed dramatically today. I've just been advised by Josh that they are ready for you in the press conference. Follow me.'

***

Turn over to read the Bonus Features Section which includes:

Bravo Two Eleven M.I.S.T. Season 1

Introduction

Episode 1 – Zombie Horde

Episode 2 – Battle Royale Squads

Episode 3 – Middle East Deployment

<u>Bravo Two Eleven, Origins</u>

Novel Blurb

Bonus Features Section

10 Regiment

Bravo Two Eleven

M.I.S.T.

Season One

A.I. James

Blurb

Bravo Two Eleven, M.I.S.T. Series, Season 1

Release date: September 29, 2018.
Word Count: 37,540
Written by: A.I. James
Style: Short story collections

Description: Join Chris and the rest of her tactical team, Bravo Two Eleven, as they hone their skills using the Memoreyes Immersive Simulation Training where months inside M.I.S.T. are mere seconds in the real world. Deployments include scenarios such as Battle Royale, Counter-Terrorism, Police Assistance, Conventional Warfare...oh and zombies, battling with and against citizens with superpowers, alien invasion and anything else the programmers can think of to push them to their limits.

Introduction

Fiona stood at the window of the command room and looked down at the pods below. It had taken the Allied Intelligence Agency less than eight hours following the fall of Sapho to position the seven hundred and twenty-one pods into the warehouse and link them to the server. It was an impressive feat to accomplish the task considering this phase of M.I.S.T. wasn't expected to be online for at least another six months. The pods, originally designed in this quantity for full regimental tactical simulations remained as a theoretical concept, until the first tactical team had entered the simulator and reported their findings, but the events of the day had forced their hand.

Fiona removed the chaos crystal from around her neck that had shielded her thoughts and the truth from the students with telepathic abilities. After surviving the tragedy of losing an entire planet, the gifted Sapho citizens, both adults and children, were led into the warehouse and instructed to climb into the pods. The children were understandably terrified when the glass ceiling of the pods closed above them, sealing them inside, after all, this was the first piece of technology they'd seen in their life and the majority were still in shock from becoming orphans only hours earlier. The sound of the younger children's screams and their thumping hands against the glass until the sleeping gas entered the pods will stay with her forever.

The teams of medical and computer technicians then opened the pods and prepared each body for sustained living in a sedated state. Their consciousness was paused. The truth was, the computer scientists had no program prepared for an event like this which was something they were working furiously to overcome.

Fiona turned to her right as she saw the Director approaching her in the reflection of the window.

'It's been quite a day,' said the Director.

It was the biggest understatement Fiona had ever heard but was typical of the Director's nature. It was reassuring that not even the collapse of a planet could shake the person in charge of the Allied Intelligence Agency and by default, in charge of 10 Regiment.

'Quite a day, indeed, Sir.'

'What's their status?'

'They are in limbo, paused without a consciousness.'

'And the programmers?'

'They've converted an Allied city from the tactical M.I.S.T. simulator they've named Mistopolis. It's almost ready for non-tactical inhabitants.'

'Good,' said the director nodding his head. 'See to it that the programmers populate it with a realistic blend of citizens, keep a lot of the hostile elements so it mirrors our own cities.'

'Yes, Sir. What's next for them?'

'I think it's important to be honest with them. When we bring them into the M.I.S.T. program, we'll tell them they're in an accelerated learning simulator. We'll gather the surviving gifted academy instructors and complete their studies in their gift as best as we can and then we'll run them through the Earth assimilation program. Once they've graduated, we're going to test them.'

'Test them for what, Sir?'

The Director considered the question before answering.

'Everything. The gifted were never meant to permanently live in our world, in fact, in our regiment's history, I can count the gifted visitors to Earth on a single hand. I want them to remember each evolution, to learn from every experience so they can apply what they've learnt from the assimilation training and ultimately live in the real world and blend in when this is all over. I see only three pathways for the gifted once the simulations have been completed. I need M.I.S.T. to analyze which ones can be safely released into the real world without being a threat to Earth's citizens, which ones have what it takes to be trained as a gifted specialist for missions in 10 Regiment and which ones are so dangerous that they will never be woken from their pod. I'll leave the finer details for you to work out.'

A chill ran up Fiona's spine. If the gifted citizens in front of her failed the simulations, the pods she had urged them to lay in would become their prison cell.

The director turned away from Fiona. He took four steps towards the door and stopped.

'Fiona, I want the tactical program to proceed as we've previously discussed. The arrival of the gifted changes nothing in regard to what M.I.S.T. was originally designed for. Pull Bravo Two Eleven from the active duty roster, give them a week off and then run them through the mission packages. Out of all the teams, I think they'll get the most benefit from it.'

'Yes, Sir.'

M.I.S.T. Episode 1

Author: A.I. James

Development Team Update

Hi Agents,

We've developed a simulator within 10 Regiment that will become a major part of the game. Go to the in-game HQ and sign-up for the closed M.I.S.T. Beta Test group if you want to experience missions that you won't find anywhere else, try out the new skins, new weapons and new game dynamics.

Enjoy.

Jeremy

Creative Director

10 Regiment

Episode 1.1

Jack lifted the disc hanging from the silver chain around Chris's neck.

'That's different. Where did you get it?'

Chris sighed internally, whilst smiling externally. She was exactly 46 minutes into the blind date Brooke had organized against her will, despite Chris's graphic threats of harm if she went ahead with it. It's not that there was anything wrong with Jack, he just wasn't Alec…or Ash for that matter, but on the plus side, Jack wasn't a secret 10 Regiment agent either so, as far as her recently created moral code dictated, she could at least date him, but for those very same reasons, she couldn't tell him a single thing about the disc around her neck.

'I got it after going through hell and making it back alive.'

'Oh, now you have to tell me the story!'

'I'm joking. It's like one my Dad wore. Wearing it reminds me we have something in common.'

'When did he leave?'

Chris's muscles tensed.

'He didn't leave. He would never leave. He died during military service.'

'Sorry. That was a stupid thing to assume. My Dad left when I was four, never saw him again. How is the disc getting warmer? It looks too thin to have batteries inside it?'

Chris pulled the disc from Jack's grasp. He was right. The disc was heating up. She had been activated.

'RIPPLE - BRACE, BRACE, BRACE!' yelled a waitress facing the window looking out onto the street.

Chris and Jack slid off their chairs, taking cover underneath their table. The room warped, stretching and contracting as the six-foot-high ripple passed through the restaurant.

Jack looked up at Chris. 'I've never experienced a ripple like that before.'

'I have, once before. Nothing good ever follows a ripple like that. Sorry, Jack, I have to go,' said Chris standing up and placing enough money on the table to cover the date.

'I don't want your money.'

'Well, then the waitress will appreciate the tip.'

'Chris, don't leave. It might not be safe.'

'It's because it might not be safe that I have to leave. Bye, Jack.'

Chris walked away without ever looking back as other people in the restaurant began to come out from under their tables. Five minutes later, she was turning into her driveway. Chris got out of her car as the garage door closed.

'Agent 1940 – Abracadabra.'

A wormhole began to form next to her. She stepped through it into the first level of 10 Regiment's subterranean headquarters. Fiona was waiting for her.

'Hi, Chris.'

'Hi, Fi,' said Chris, giving her friend a hug.

'Were you on a date?'

'Not a good one. What's happened? We just had a huge ripple. It felt the same as when ELIP-1 was destroyed.'

'We're investigating the origin of that ripple, but your team won't be involved in that. I've got another task for you. Relax, it's not a mission...well...not really.'

'Okay, now I'm worried.'

Fiona laughed. She pushed the radio depressor switch on the front of her body armor.

'TOC, this is Fi, connect the server on the level one wormhole wall to receiver 28635.'

'Fi, this is TOC, acknowledged.'

Chris glanced behind her at the wormhole forming on the wall which was guarded by a heavily armed agent in each corner. She turned back to Fiona.

'You're deploying me without any weapons or equipment? Dressed like this?'

'The Research and Development Team have built a simulator. Bravo Two Eleven is the first tactical team to try it out. The rest of your team is already there.'

'How long will I be deployed?'

'It's only for one week…in our time.'

'In our time? What's that supposed to mean?'

'You have trust issues, Chris. Has anyone ever told you that? Turn around and walk through the wormhole. I'll see you in a week,' said Fiona, giving her a little wave. Fiona turned and vanished through the wormhole under the sign, Sector Two.

Chris turned and walked through the wormhole on the back wall wearing the dress and heels from the date with nothing more than a clutch purse in her hand to defend herself with.

Episode 1.2

Chris stepped out of the wormhole and into a room that terrified her. Her team were standing only two feet in front of her looking as equally nervous as she felt. None had ventured too far away from the wormhole that brought them to this place.

To her right was a small theatre with tiered seating and a large smart-glass panel at the front. To her left were six horizontal pods, three on either side of the room that were large enough to fit a human inside. The wall beyond the pods was a large mirror which Chris would bet her life on it being a two-way mirror like the ones in the questioning rooms back in headquarters. Directly in front of her was a dark hallway that somehow felt more ominous than the pods.

'Good evening, Agents. Please take a seat in the theatre,' requested a man appearing from the darkened hallway.

Chris led the way to the front row. To Chris's horror, every other agent sat in the row behind her...just in case.

'Welcome to M.I.S.T. My name is Josh Sapho, I'm the lead engineer on this project. You're the first team through this facility so we are wrapped to see you and to finally be operational. Can I please ask you to state your name and position?'

'Christine Whittaker, everyone calls me Chris, Bravo Two Eleven Team Leader. On the night of the red crystal raid, weren't you where the scientist from level four who handed Damon and Sage that faulty C-bomb. That didn't end too well for them, did it?'

Josh swallowed…twice.

'That was…unfortunate…full disclosure, I told them before they deployed that we hadn't field tested anything their team used during that mission.'

'So, is this place, going to end like that night?' asked Chris.

'This place is going to blow your mind…sorry, bad choice of words.'

Josh looked at the agents behind Chris.

'Alec Darcy – Assault Team, second-in-charge.'

'Zach Jennings – Assault Team, point man and all-round bad-ass.'

'Terrence Merreweather – Assault Team, Method of Entry expert.'

'Ash Sapho – Sniper Team Leader.'

'Owen Sapho – Sniper Team, second-in-charge and healer.'

'Sniper Team only has two people, second-in-charge is like saying you got second in a two-person race,' joked Ash.

Josh looked at the sniper team.

'I didn't realize this team had anyone from Sapho. This just makes today even better.'

'Josh, can you explain what we are doing here?' asked Chris.

'This is the future for 10 Regiment training. M.I.S.T. is short for Memoreyes Immersive Simulation Training. The short explanation of M.I.S.T. is we get a team of agents, that's you, we connect some electrodes to your head and put you to sleep inside those pods and then we run any kind of training simulation we want. Seconds in real life transfer to months when you're deployed in the simulator, just like when you dream at night. We can drill you in every kind of tactical scenario we can think of, change the environment or crank up the difficulty whilst you're in the simulator and we can even record your missions for group debriefing. The best part is, when we wake you up from the pods, you'll remember everything you've gone through. In one week's time, you'll be the most elite tactical agents in the world.'

'News flash champ, we already are the most elite agents in the world,' said Zach.

'So, what you're saying is we are going to be inside a computer game?' asked Chris.

'That's exactly what I'm saying,' confirmed Josh.

'Everything you just said, I'm all in. When can we start?' asked Alec.

'If you're that keen, we can start immediately.'

Chris looked around the room, the boys were salivating at the thought of being inside a computer game. She turned to Josh.

'Were in, let's go.'

'Okay, every game has rules, this one is no different. At the start of each game, sorry, each mission, you'll begin at your start point, which is a purple circle on the ground that surrounds the team. You all need to step outside the circle to disarm the start point and commence the mission. The team will have one crystal to carry with you. Place it on the ground and push the button to activate the crystal. When you're in the simulator, you'll have a display strapped to your non-dominant forearm. You'll be able to configure through several screens such as the mission map, the mission objective and the armory. The most important part of your display is the health bar at the top, green is good, yellow is not good and red means you're approaching death. You will feel pain in the simulator, but your real-life bodies will remain unharmed. If you get injured, miss a meal, run out of water or skip sleep, your health will be affected, just like in the real world. If you die'

'Wait, what?'

'Shut-up, Chris, this is epic! Keep going,' said Zach.

'If you die, depending on the mission parameters, you'll either return to this room and follow the mission in spectator mode or you will be respawned at your last crystal as a team when the last agent in your team dies. As far as weapons go, we'll fit you out with the weapons available within the regiment for the type of mission you're deploying on. Given that you're our first team to go through the training, we'll also give you some of our experimental weapons to try out and for our own analysis, we may just make things up as we go and get inventive. We do have sponsors that help fund this training so at times, we'll let them dictate some of the parameters. We weren't expecting you to want to jump straight into the simulator, so we haven't got a specific mission loaded up into the server yet, but we have a library of missions you can select from. I'm open to suggestions since you're the first team to enter M.I.S.T.

'If anyone says anything other than zombie horde, I will punch you in the face,' said Zach.

Josh looked at Chris for guidance.

Chris looked at the agents in her team and sighed.

'I guess we're picking zombie horde.'

'YEAH!' roared the boys behind Chris.

Episode 1.3

Chris climbed into her pod and rolled onto her back. The technician assigned to her pod connected electrodes to either side of her forehead.

'I'm all done. Just relax,' said the technician in a soothing tone.

'I'd be more relaxed if my team wasn't obsessed with fighting zombies. Why couldn't they pick going to a park filled with puppies for the first simulation?'

The technician smiled.

'We are going to clear the room. In a few minutes, a vapor will enter the pod and you'll fall asleep. We'll see you in a week. Good luck.'

Chris flinched as the glass ceiling of the pod lowered over the top of her. A cool, gentle breeze from behind her passed over her head. She turned her head to see the other agents in her team smiling like maniacs' moments before her eyes closed.

***

Chris opened her eyes. She had no memory of how she came to be in the room with no doors or windows, just concrete on every surface except for the wall directly in front of her which was made from smart-glass. Her team were all standing inside a purple circle marked onto the floor.

'This isn't what I expected when I requested a zombie horde,' said Zach.

Large writing appeared on the screen.

Standby for simulation.

Gift not enabled.

A countdown started on the wall.

5, 4, 3, 2, 1, 0

The floor dropped away from under Chris's feet. She squeezed her eyes. Her stomach pushed against the back of her throat. Then it was over. Chris opened her eyes. She was standing in the middle of a forest dressed in her black counter-terrorism uniform.

'Wow,' said Alec, emitting a small cloud of vapor into the chilled air.

'Sssh,' whispered Owen, pointing into the distance at a lone zombie wearing ripped brown pants and a dirty red t-shirt stumbling through the trees.

Chris dropped instinctively to her knees. She slid the M4 that was slung over her shoulder into her hands. She checked the pistol strapped to her thigh, it was already loaded.

One by one, her team checked their weapons and equipment.

Chris looked at the device strapped to her left forearm. Her health bar along the top of the screen was full and green. At bottom of the screen on the left was the words, Attempt #1. On the right was Difficulty 2/5. In the center of the screen was a map showing the forest with a building surrounded by cliffs on all four sides located to the north. She touched a tab at the side of the map titled, Mission Objective.

Locate the building. One person must hit the red button, then hit the blue button to be extracted.

'Seems simple enough,' said Terrence, looking over Chris's shoulder at her display, even though he had his own.

'Don't bother checking the armory tab, there's nothing in it,' said Zach, a little disappointed.

'There's got to be a catch,' said Ash.

'You ready to go find these buttons?' asked Chris.

Her team all raised their thumb.

'Let's move out,' said Chris, pointing in the direction of the building. 'Zach, you're on point.'

'I want to go kill that zombie over there,' whispered Zach pointing in the other direction.

Chris sighed.

'Seriously, Zach?'

'I'll just do one, then we can go the way you want.'

'Fine, but be careful, don't make any noise.'

'You got it,' said Zach.

Chris led her team out of the purple protective circle and covered Zach's approach towards the zombie who seemed completely oblivious to its impending doom.

Zach switched from normal...well, as normal as Zach can be, into predator mode as easily as other people breathe. He stalked the zombie, walking on the outside of his feet and rolling them into the forest floor as he transitioned his weight silently onto each foot, carefully avoiding anything that would make noise and alert the zombie of his presence. Once Zach had circled around the zombie to approach it from behind, he moved in for the kill.

Chris followed Zach's movement through the red dot sight on her M4. Zach withdrew a throwing knife from the front of his body armor that Chris hadn't even noticed was there and raised it behind his head. It was about to happen.

'I've got eyes on, Zach. Terrence, cover his North. Owen, cover his South, Alec, cover his East, Ash, cover his West,' whispered Chris.

Zach was close enough to hear the zombie's labored breathing. The parts of its skin Zach could see was torn and sagging and looked in various stages of decay. It almost felt like putting it out of its misery was the right thing to do...almost. He tightened his grip on the handle of the knife and lunged forward. The tip of the blade barely met any resistance as it penetrated the zombie's rotting skull and lodged deep inside its brain. The zombie groaned and fell to its knees, then slumped face forward into the dirt.

Chris relaxed, exhaling the breath she had been unconsciously holding. She continued to watch Zach through her weapon's sight. Zach looked at the zombie and then turned towards her. He looked like he'd been cheated, as though the experience was nothing like what his childhood fantasy had envisioned.

'Seriously? That's it?' said Zach, raising his hands in the air, no longer feeling compelled to whisper due to such a pathetic enemy.

'BOOM!'

The zombie exploded.

Everything within two yards of the zombie was blown to pieces. Trees, plants, a flying bird with the world's worst timing...and Zach.

'Ooocha...ooooocha.'

Chris spun towards a noise directly behind her. Alec was on his hands and knees, projectile vomiting. Chris placed a hand on Alec's back and rubbed him like he was a puppy.

'Remember everyone, it's just a game. He'll be respawned.'

'BEST. GAME. EVER!' said Terrence smiling.

Chris pushed the sight of Zach exploding into hundreds of bits from her mind and remembered this was a tactical simulation that was being recorded. She raised her M4 back to her shoulder.

'Check your areas, what's our status?'

'Clear to the North,' whispered Terrence.

'Clear to the South, whispered Owen.

'Clear to the East,' whispered Alec, wiping his chin with his sleeve and noticing his health bar had dropped slightly after vomiting.

'Clear to the West,' whispered Ash.

Chris looked at the map on her screen. It was obvious what they had to do. She ignored Terrence's sudden rise in spirits. 'Alec, you're on point. Move out,' said Chris, pointing in the direction of the cliffs even though she couldn't see any sign of them yet.

The team wound their way through the trees, at times, going well off course to avoid confronting any more zombies stumbling aimlessly through the forest. Alec carefully advanced on his bearing, repeating the same process of scanning for zombies, taking a dozen steps and then scanning the distance once again. He stopped next to a boulder that was the height of his hip and knelt behind it. Ahead of him was a largest concentration of zombies he'd seen so far. He turned back to Chris and motioned with his hands for her to join him.

'What do you think?' he asked.

'There must be a few hundred at least,' said Chris scanning the horde of zombies dressed identical to the zombie that had killed Zach. 'I guess we can't avoid them forever. I don't get it though, if the cliffs are as high as what they seem on my display, we should be almost on top of them, or at the very least, we should be able to see them by now,' replied Chris.

'So, push through then?' asked Alec, wanting Chris to saying anything, but yes.

'Yes, push through,' she said. She pushed her radio pressure switch on her body armor. 'Listen up team, we're heading through a horde. Keep your movements slow and only engage if you are under immediate threat.'

Chris nodded to Alec. Alec reluctantly stood up and stepped forward.

The forest exploded in front of Alec.

'TAKE COVER!' yelled Chris, diving to the ground.

A cliff the size of a city skyscraper erupted from the dirt twenty yards in front of the team, by the time the cliff stopped ascending, Chris couldn't see the top of it anymore, but that wasn't the part that scared her. Directly in front of her was a tunnel that could fit a train inside it leading into the center of the cliffs where the building was located.

'This doesn't look good,' whispered Ash.

Chris agreed. Despite the zombies not even flinching at the sudden appearance of the cliffs, there was a sense of foreboding seeping out of the trees. Chris kept her eyes on the tunnel entrance as her shaking left hand fumbled for the Velcro flap on the pouch that contained her team's one and only saving crystal. She slowly ripped the Velcro apart.

Alec turned to see what the sound was and nodded. 'Good call. If I've learnt anything from years of gaming, things about to get serious.'

Chris grasped the purple crystal and removed it from the pouch. She placed the crystal into the dirt and pressed the small button on the top of it. It was now operational.

'I'll take point through the tunnel?' said Chris.

Without saying another word, Chris stood up and walked towards the tunnel's entrance. Something was moving inside the tunnel. She held her left hand up with her fingers extended. Her team stopped behind her and propped onto one knee, whilst simultaneously raising their weapons to their shoulder. Chris pushed her radio pressure switch.

'Zombies inside the tunnel. No-one engages unless they attack you first. Copy?' whispered Chris.

One by one, the team acknowledged her order.

Chris stood up and stepped inside the darkness. She approached the first zombie. It was clawing at the dirt, dragging its motionless legs behind it. Another ten zombies were behind it, shuffling along the wall of the tunnel. She was just out of arm's reach from it though still close enough for it to turn its head at her and hiss a warning not to come any closer. It was female and Chris briefly wondered whether it had once been a human or had it always been a zombie. It was only after that thought that Chris remembered that even though she seemed real, she was inside a game and game characters didn't have a past, a back story, or feelings or thoughts for that matter. Repeating to herself that this was just a game helped her edge past the zombies that were standing and walking. The last zombie within the tunnel slowly turned towards her and hissed which made her jog for a few steps to get away from it.

Chris stepped out of the tunnel and into the interior chamber the cliffs had concealed. She stopped and waited for her team to join her, each agent had managed to hold their nerve and make it through the tunnel without incident.

'Can anyone say trap?' asked Ash.

Chris was thinking the same thing. The area inside the cliffs was roughly two football fields long and one field wide. The blue button was in front of her in the middle of the short wall to her right. All the way down the other end of the chamber, was a concrete building, two levels high. Between the blue button and the building was scattered rocks and the horde of zombies Alec had shown Chris minutes earlier before the cliffs appeared.

'Hisssss'

'THUD!'

Chris spun around. A zombie was falling backwards in front of Terrence who had just smashed the zombie's face with the butt of his M4 by the looks of how he was holding his weapon. He looked at Chris.

'Are we spreading out or going as a group?' asked Terrence.

'Let's stick together.'

The closer the team got to the building, the more the zombies took an interest in the agents. They had covered half the distance to the building when the horde's behavior suddenly changed.

'I don't think we can go much further like this,' warned Chris. There just isn't enough space to weave through them. Is everyone ready to make a break for the building?'

'We've been ready since we came out of the tunnel,' said Ash.

'Bunch up. Stay close together. The second we fire, sprint towards the house. Fire at will on three, two, one….GO!'

'CRACK, CRACK, CRACK, CRACK, CRACK.'

A hole opened in the horde in front of them.

'RUN! Keep shooting!' yelled Chris.

Chris ran faster than she ever thought possible. She jumped over the fallen zombies and continued to shoot more in front of her.

'CRACK, CRACK!'

Then it happened.

'BOOM!'

A zombie exploded. Chris didn't dare turn around. She shot the last zombie blocking her from the building and emptied the rest of her magazine into the window next to the door.

'CRACK, CRACK, CRACK, CRACK, CRACK, CRACK.'

She dove head-first through the shattered window, slammed into the floor, rolled onto her back, drew her pistol from the holster on her thigh and aimed it at the window as the chain reaction of exploding zombies spread.

'BOOM, BOOM, BOOM, BOOM, BOOM, BOOM, BOOM, BOOM, BOOM, BOOM, BOOM, BOOM, BOOM, BOOM, BOOM, BOOM, BOOM.'

Alec appeared through the window, then Ash...Chris waited for the rest of her team to appear, but they never did.

'BOOM, BOOM.'

Chris propped herself up onto her knees. She peeked over the edge of the window. The compound was clear.

'Cover me,' ordered Chris.

Alec, stood up and raised his weapon. 'Covering.'

Chris changed her magazine in her M4. She looked up at Alec to tell him to change his magazine for fully loaded one when she saw it.

'Alec, your health bar!'

Alec rolled his wrist so he could see his display.

'I thought that might happen.'

'But why?' asked Chris. She didn't want to lose him too, game or not. She wanted Alec by her side.

Alec pulled his collar, exposing the left side of his neck and shoulder. Blood oozed out of multiple zombie bites and lacerations.

'They got me just before I dove through the window.'

'How much time do you think you have?'

Alec looked at his display. 'Enough time to find that red button and cover you to the blue button so we can get out of this sim.'

'Found the red button,' said Ash, looking at the back wall of the building.

'Great. Chris, hit it and run. We'll cover you,' said Alec.

'Just a second. I don't want to have to do that again,' said Chris. She pushed the flashing crystal on the map on her display. A pop-up text box appeared.

Retrieve?

She pushed retrieve and raised her right hand. A purple crystal slammed into the palm of her hand. She placed it on the floor and pushed the button. The crystal activated. Chris walked over to the red button.

'Are you ready?' asked Chris.

'We're ready,' replied Ash and Alec, propping themselves up on the wall with their weapons resting on the window sill.

'Do it,' said Alec.

Chris stood next to the red button that was made from solid steel. She pushed it and was surprised by how easily it slid backwards until it clicked. Chris pulled the door open, angry at herself for not opening the door before hitting the button and losing vital seconds. She ran into the chamber. Screams erupted from behind her. She glanced over her shoulder. Alec and Ash were fighting zombies in hand to hand combat and these zombies were anything but slow and docile. She turned her head back in the direction she was running and immediately stopped. A wall of zombies wearing green shirts were sprinting out of the tunnel. Within seconds, they had blocked the blue button and were now running directly at her, at least thirty rows deep. They were less than forty yards from her. Ash and Alec fell silent behind her. Chris dropped to one knee, raised her M4 and killed as many as she could before they reached her.

'CRACK, CRACK, CRACK, CRACK, CRACK.......'

Episode 1.4

'Urgh!'

Chris opened her eyes. She was sitting within the purple circle inside the building. Her entire team were with her.

'Okay, does anyone want to tell me what happened?' said Zach.

'The zombie you killed exploded, that's what killed you,' said Owen.

'All the red shirt zombies explode, not just the one Zach killed,' said Terrence.

'Such a crap way to die,' spat Zach. 'So how did you all die?'

'I'll take this one,' said Chris. 'Quick recap for everyone. We're inside what appears to be a chamber which is bordered on all four sides with cliffs. There's only one way in and out which is the tunnel we came through, oh and Zach, the cliffs just appeared out of nowhere. There were hundreds of red shirt zombies between us and the building we are currently in. We got through most of them, but then had to clear the rest of the way, which started a chain reaction of explosions. That's where we lost Owen and Terrence. The red button is on the wall behind us. Alec was infected by the zombies and losing health fast. I hit the button and ran out of the building. That's when it happened.'

'What happened? Please say zombie horde,' said Zach, leaning in closer like he was a child being told a magical story.

'When the red button is pushed, the zombies change to green shirts and they run faster and are more aggressive than anything I've ever seen in my life. Alec and Ash got hit from behind by zombies which must be inside this building. I was half way across the compound when hundreds of zombies rushed through the tunnel and ran straight at me.'

'And what did you do?' asked Zach.

'I dropped to my knee and shot as many as I could as they rushed me.'

Zach sighed. 'Oh my god, you died alone while facing down a full zombie horde. You're so lucky.'

'If they're as fast as you say they are, how are we going to hit the blue button after the red button?' asked Owen.

'I'm not sure, how about sniper team clears the windows so we can use the building as cover while the assault team takes care of the zombies upstairs?'

'Sounds good to me,' said Ash.

Chris looked at the other team members. Everyone agreed with the plan.

'Okay, lets go,' said Chris, releasing the crystal.

Zach and Alec led the way up the stairs and stacked up on the closed door. Chris followed behind them. Terrence removed the snake camera from the front of his body armor and fed the camera head under the door. He scanned the room, left to right and then retrieved the camera.

'Three zombies, all red shirts,' whispered Terrence.

'Get in, take the shot and get out of the room,' said Chris. She pushed her radio pressure switch.

'Sniper team, we're about to engage three red shirt zombies. Move to the windows in case it triggers the horde.'

'Sniper team, acknowledged,' replied Ash.

Chris waited for Terrence to stow his camera into the pouch on his body armor and then squeezed Alec's shoulder, who then squeezed Zach's shoulder. Zach stood up and raised his thumb. Terrence stepped forward and kicked the door open.

Zach raised his M4, entered the room and turned to the left.

'CRACK!'

Alec and Chris split to the center and to the right.

'CRACK, CRACK!'

'GO, GO, GO!'

Chris waited for Alec and Zach to run back through the doorway before she dove for the cover of the stairwell.

'BOOM, BOOM, BOOM!'

Chris pushed her radio pressure switch. 'Sniper team, are we clear?'

'All clear, zero horde.'

Chris stood up and walked back into the room. The blue button remained unguarded at the other end of the compound, but she knew it wouldn't stay that way for long. She turned and walked back downstairs. The rest of her team were removing all their magazines from the pouches on their body armor and stacking them on the windows sills.

Ash looked over at Chris.

'We've been thinking about a last stand kind of scenario to see if the horde only has a certain number or whether they keep coming.'

'So, no-one is trying to hit the blue button?' asked Chris.

Ash shrugged. 'If this works, then all we have to do is protect the person who hit the button and then they can walk up to the button once the horde is cut down.'

'Who is being protected?' asked Chris.

'I was thinking you,' said Alec. 'I don't think I can see you die like this.'

'What! Are we in the 1950's?' asked Chris. She scanned the team. Everyone seemed too excited about the impending horde to sit it out, especially Zach and there was only one person that would listen to her without arguing. 'Owen, you'll push the button and then go upstairs and wait it out. Hopefully after this is over, we'll come up and get you.'

'Okay,' said Owen, walking over to the red button. 'Tell me when you're ready.'

Chris joined her team and placed her magazines on the window sill.

'Ready?' asked Chris.

'I've never been more excited about anything in my life!' said Zach.

Chris turned to Owen and nodded.

'Pushing the button in three, two, one…now!'

'Here they come!' squealed Zach.

'Fire at will!' ordered Chris.

The team opened fire.

'CRACK, CRACK, CRACK, CRACK, CRACK, CRACK, CRACK, CRACK, CRACK, CRACK, CRACK, CRACK, CRACK, CRACK, CRACK, CRACK, CRACK, CRACK, CRACK, CRACK.'

The front two rows of zombies fell, but the horde continued to advance.

'KEEP FIRING!' yelled Chris.

'CRACK, CRACK.'

The horde were seconds away from the building. Zach stood up with a knife in each hand. He leapt through the shattered window and disappeared into the horde. The team backed up from the front of the building as the zombies flooded the room.

'CRACK, CRACK, CRACK, CRACK, CRACK, CRACK, CRACK, CRACK, CRACK, CRACK, CRACK, CRACK, CRACK, CRACK, CRACK, CRACK, CRACK...'

Owen aimed his M4 at the open doorway. He'd watched the horde fill the chamber and run relentlessly towards the building. Seconds after he lost sight of the front of the horde, the shooting from his team had been silenced. He could hear their rushed footsteps up stairwell. He had seconds to live. As he contemplated being torn apart, a moment of inspiration hit him. The first zombie appeared in the doorway. He turned away from the zombie and fired across the compound at the blue button.

'CRACK, CRACK.'

His shots dropped the zombie in front of the button. A hand grabbed his shoulder.

'CRACK!'

Owen was knocked off his feet. The room blurred. He realized he was still alive and opened his eyes. He was laying on the floor of the concrete room where the simulation had started. The other agents were looking around, looking just as dazed and confused as he was.

'What happened?' asked Owen.

'I think it's over,' said Chris. She turned to Owen. 'What did you do?'

'I knew you were dead when the shooting stopped. Just before the zombies got me, I remembered the mission objective: One person must hit the red button, then hit the blue button to be extracted. It never said we had to touch it…we only had to hit it.'

'So, you're saying we didn't have to get ripped apart multiple times. All we had to do was shoot the buttons?'

An image of a bald butler dressed in a tuxedo appeared on the panel of smart-glass. The butler raised his eyebrows and clapped slowly. 'Congratulations on finally passing a mission rated two out of five for difficulty. I'm sure your parents would be proud of you. Here's a mission tip: Don't make things harder for yourself than they have to be.'

The butler faded off the screen and was replaced with words:

Health and ammunition restored.

Next simulation starts in 30 seconds.

'I don't like that butler,' yelled Chris. 'Okay team, here we go again.'

M.I.S.T. Episode 2

Author: A.I. James

Episode 2.1

Health and ammunition restored.

Next simulation starts in 30 seconds.

Chris read the words on the smart glass panel as the rest of her team gathered around her inside the purple circle on the floor. The words on the screen faded. The mission parameters flashed onto the screen. Following each word were hundreds of possible answers shuffling within the answer box.

Fiona's voice emitted through the room from an unseen speaker. 'Please say stop when you are ready.'

Chris checked with her team. They all nodded.

'Stop!' said Chris.

The shuffling selections stopped.

Chris read the first line and moaned.

Mission Type: Battle Royale – Squad 10 v 10

Map: Urban

Weather: Lightening storm

Gift enabled – Specialists assigned.

Uniform: Skin sponsor - Penelope07

Start Point: Air

Chris turned to her team. 'Okay, help me out, what's a skin sponsor?'

'A skin is what you're wearing and what you look like. A skin sponsor means someone is dressing us,' said Terrence as though the words were poison in his mouth.

'Are you serious?' asked Chris.

'I'd be more concerned about the vague start point,' said Ash.

The mission parameters faded from the screen and were replaced with a word that made Chris's body tense.

BYE

Chris fell through the floor as it disappeared. She looked down and screamed.

'AARRGGGHHHH!'

Chris tumbled through the night sky between bolts of lightning, thousands of feet above the town that was built in the middle of nowhere. She stabilized her descent as a huge white rabbit flew past her, scaring her more than the lightning bolts. The rabbit looked at her and drifted close enough for her to see the look of disgust on Zach's face. He reached out and grabbed her side. Chris looked at the display on her arm and realized her arm was covered in white fur. She was also wearing a white rabbit onesie. She glanced over her shoulder. Seven rabbits flew into position behind and grabbed hold of each other's arms and legs. They were flying blindly on her guidance. Other teams were plummeting towards the town around them. Between the team in red armor and another team that looked like astronauts, they might have got off easy with the bunny suits. A moment of panic hit Chris, none of the teams she could see had parachutes. She looked down at her shoulder and chest. The were no straps, which meant a parachute wasn't on her back.

Chris watched a team below her. They were less than a thousand feet above the town. Now nine hundred feet, eight hundred feet… they broke formation. Two seconds later, tiny gliders appeared in their hands. A lightning bolt incinerated three of them.

Chris gave her team the hand signal to break formation. Her fingers wrapped around the handles of the glider. Her body jerked violently as the pathetic sized parachute attached the to the top of the glider filled with air. She worked out how to steer by pulling the handles left and right. The tiny town surrounded by a purple wall was rushing up on her. There was only a handful of buildings to choose from unless she wanted to land near a glowing chest on the street. She glanced at the surrounding air space. A team of Vikings were heading towards a two-level house. The red armored knights were heading towards a stadium while the astronauts were landing in front of a library.

Chris aimed at the tallest building. As she got closer, she could see three glowing chests scattered across the roof where she intended to land. She looked at the trees around the building and pulled the glider to the right to drift into the wind to control her rate of descent. She was perfectly aligned with the closest glowing chest as a team of super-heroes swooped in with the wind at their backs. She was ten yards above them when their feet hit the roof. The team slammed into the roof hard. Bodies tumbled across the concrete. Only their leader stayed on his feet during the landing. The same man who had led the team was now running towards the closest chest carrying a pick axe in both hands.

Chris aimed straight at him. She let go of her glider six feet above him and used his body to break her fall. A pick axe appeared in her hand. 'Sorry,' she said as she raised the axe above her head and swung it tip of it through his skull. The leader vanished.

'Not so super now, are you!' screamed Zach.

Chris turned around. Three superheroes vanished from around Zach's feet, who was breathing hard holding his own pick axe.

Terrence was in a melee with a broad-shouldered lycra wearing superhero, trading blow for blow with their axes.

CRACK, CRACK...CRACK, CRACK!

Ash shot the man in front of him and then finished off the superhero fighting Terrence.

'Rooftop clear,' he bellowed before turning back to the chest. He passed the pump shotgun and AR-15 to Owen and Alec.

Chris opened the chest closest to her and removed the pistols sitting on top of two jars with different colored liquid inside.

'HELP! BRAVO TWO ELEVEN! SOMEBODY PLEASE HELP ME!'

Chris looked over the edge of the rooftop. A female bunny was standing in the middle of the road holding an axe, she was pointing her hands at the advancing lumberjacks, but nothing was happening. She ran to the side of the street and onto the grass. The lumberjacks were closing in on her. Suddenly, dirt walls erupted from the ground between the bunny and the lumberjacks. The team of lumberjacks were knocking them down with their axes as fast as the bunny was making them. A ramp appeared in front of the bunny, then another, and another as the lumberjacks chased her into the sky.

'There's a stranded bunny over here that needs help,' yelled Chris. 'UP HERE BUNNY. COME THIS WAY.'

Her team ran to the edge of the roof Chris was looking over as she opened fire with her pistols.

CRACK, CRACK, CRACK, CRACK, CRACK, CRACK, CRACK, CRACK, CRACK!

Only one lumberjack escaped the ambush by jumping off the side of the ramp. His body vanished when he landed on the ground, killed from the fall. The bunny kept building ramps until she was on the rooftop with her team.

'Are you okay?' asked Chris.

'No...my gift, it didn't work on the black ground and then there were those people were chasing me with axes and why are we all dressed like rabbits?' said the girl looking over the edge of the building. She turned back to Chris. 'What weapons did you use against them? Wait, please tell me you're Bravo Two Eleven. This is my first mission. I've wanted to be a guardian for so long, please tell me I haven't done something wrong already? Hang on, you're a girl...are you Chris? You are, aren't you?'

Chris held up her hand. 'Relax...Yes, my name is Chris and yes, this is Bravo Two Eleven and yes, this is a hostile area so please keep your voice down. What's your name and how old are you?'

'Ruby. I'm fourteen,' whispered Ruby.

'I see you're a gifted bunny?' said Chris.

'I'm a green cloak. I can change the ground and plants.'

'Correction, you were a green cloak. No such thing anymore,' said Ash.

'Yeah, sorry, that's what I meant.'

Chris extended her hand. 'Quick team introduction, that's Ash, Alec, Terrence, Owen and Zach.'

'I'm Hannah,' said another bunny squatting next to the third chest on the roof.

'Hannah, sorry, I didn't see you had joined us,' said Chris.

Hannah blushed and looked directly at Ash. 'I feel the same way. Oh, and Chris, this is her first Earth sim, so this might be a bit confronting for her.' Hannah turned back to Ruby. 'He's not interested so don't even ask.'

'Ash? As in the Ash of 10 Regiment?' Ruby was suddenly in awe.

Hannah stood up from the chest with a sniper rifle. 'Yes, he is the Ash of 10 Regiment. He's also the Ash of 10 Regiment who has a huge crush on the Hannah of 10 Regiment, which is me.' Hannah turned towards Ash. 'If you ever get the courage to ask me out again, I will say yes.' Hannah froze as she stared at Ruby. Her eye fixed in the one position.

'What?' asked Ruby, looking self-consciously at her bunny suit.

'EVERYONE DUCK!' yelled Hannah.

SWOOSH..............................**BOOM**

A rocket flew over the rooftop and exploded into the mountain on the other side of town.

Chris looked at Ruby who was laying on the rooftop next to her. 'She's an insanely gifted mind reader. It's weird. Just go with it.'

'We're still in a fight to the death, just in case any of you forgot,' said Terrence.

'Right, take everything out of the chests. Let's see what we've got....and stay low,' ordered Chris.

The team looked at the pile of weapons and jars of liquid. Chris picked up two of the jars of liquid. 'What do you think they do?' asked Hannah.

'Let's try them,' said Zach.

'Not until we're sure they won't hurt us,' asked Chris.

Ruby held out her hand towards Chris. 'I've already lost half of my health bar from hitting the side of the building when I was landing, so I'll try one.' She picked up the largest jar with the greenish blue liquid inside and drank it.

'How do you feel?' asked Chris.

'Great,' said Ruby. She checked her display. Her health bar was full and above it was a full blue bar that said shield.

Owen picked up a jar with brown liquid inside it and raised it to his lips. He swallowed a mouthful and collapsed. His body vanished. Only a pump shotgun lay on the ground where Owen had previously stood.

'Okay, new rule, only drink the bluey green ones,' said Zach.

'There goes our healer,' said Alec.

Ruby turned to Alec. 'You had a healer…and you let me drink the juice to maybe heal myself or maybe kill myself!'

'Probably should tell you that Ash can also heal people,' said Alec.

'I've heard Ash can do anything,' said Ruby.

CRACK!

Everyone turned towards the gunshot.

'Hannah!' yelled Chris.

'My bad, I didn't realize the trigger was so sensitive.'

Ruby looked down at her display. Her blue bar was gone and her health bar was in the red. She glared at Hannah. 'You did that on purpose! Why is everyone shooting me today?'

'Will you-?' asked Ash.

'Of course, I will go out with you,' said Hannah.

'Okay, that was equal parts beautiful and demented,' said Chris.

'Ssssssssh,' said Zach, pointing at his feet.

Footsteps were running across the floor on the level below them. The footsteps stopped. More footsteps came running in the direction the first group had come from.

DAT, DAT, DAT, DAT, DAT, DAT, DAT, DAT, DAT, DAT, DAT, DAT, DAT, BOOM, DAT, DAT, DAT, BOOM!

The battle was over.

Chris looked at Ash. 'Do you think you can blow up the roof?' she whispered.

Ash bent down and touched it. He looked up at Chris and nodded.

'Ruby, are you weapon's qualified, explosive's qualified, urban tactic's qualified?' asked Chris.

'I can use a sword.'

Chris sighed. 'Earth weapons. Are you skilled in Earth weapons or tactics?'

'No, sorry.'

'Okay. Ruby, you're with me. Everyone else, kill circle around Ash,' whispered Chris as distant battles erupted throughout the town.

The team surrounded Ash as he waited for the signal from Chris.

Chris nodded.

Ash's left hand began to glow red. He touched the roof.

BOOM!

The team dropped through the roof. Three men and a woman dressed in life guard swimsuits were looting the equipment left behind from the team they had just killed. Chris and Zach were the closest agents to the trio.

CRACK, CRACK, CRACK, CRACK, CRACK!

The lifeguards disappeared without firing a shot.

Hannah spun around. 'CHRIS LOOKOUT!'

Chris turned towards Hannah. A flash of green flew through the open window. Chris's body jerked to the left. She disappeared before her body hit the wooden floorboards.

'What was that?' asked Ash.

'Some kind of energy bullet,' said Hannah.

'What like a laser?' asked Zach.

Terrence peeked through the open window. A team of storm troopers were standing at the top of a stone fort that hadn't been there when they dropped into the town. 'Someone in their team can build forts.'

'DOWN' yelled Hannah.

A barrage of green laser bursts flew towards the building. The wall absorbed most of the damage before it disappeared. The team were completely exposed.

'I've had enough of this,' said Zach, crawling across the floor to the pile of equipment from the two fallen teams. He pushed himself to his knees and lifted a rocket launcher to his shoulder as another barrage of green laser flew towards him. He pulled the trigger. The rocket and the energy bursts crossed mid-flight.

BOOM!

The top of the tower exploded as the energy bursts entered the hallway Bravo Two Eleven were stranded in. A white membrane wall appeared in front of the team and absorbed the lasers.

Ash felt faint. He looked down at his display. The force field he summoned to shield the team had taken all but the last sliver of his health bar. Ruby ran over to him carrying a small glass canister of bluey green liquid. She raised it to Ash's lips. Ash swallowed it in one gulp. Hannah's eyes switched from Ash's slowly rising health bar to the woman who still held a jar to her boyfriend's lips with one hand and Ash's left hand in the other.

'You seriously need to be more careful,' warned Hannah…looking at Ruby rather than Ash.

Ruby let Ash's hand go.

'Um…we need to move,' said Zach.

Ash sat up. The purple wall was rapidly consuming the town. 'Downstairs, now!'

The team got to their feet and ran down the stairs. Two floors down, the purple wall entered the building and advanced up the hallway towards the staircase.

'The stairs are too slow. We're not going to make it,' yelled Terrence.

'Yes, we are,' said Ash as both of hands glowed bright red. He touched the wall.

BOOM!

The purple wall was five yards away.

'RUBY,' yelled Ash. 'Can you build us a ramp?'

Ruby ran to the edge of the hallway and looked down. There was grass on the ground below. She held out her hands as the ground began to rise towards her.

'Ruby, you've got to stop,' yelled Hannah. 'Your health bar is almost gone.'

'The ramp is still too far away. The jump onto it would kill Ash. He's more important than I am.' She raised the ramp higher and disappeared.

Ash led the team down the ramp and onto the ground. He checked his display. They were one of the last two teams remaining.

DAT!

A bullet tore through Ash's fur and into his chest.

'NO!' yelled Hannah as she ran through Ash's vanishing body.

DAT, DAT, DAT, DAT, **DAT**, DAT, DAT, DAT, DAT, DAT, DAT, DAT, DAT, **DAT**, DAT, DAT, DAT, DAT, DAT, **DAT**, DAT, DAT, DAT, DAT, DAT, DAT, DAT, DAT, **DAT**, DAT, DAT!

Bullets ripped up the turf around the team.

'I'm hit,' yelled Terrence.

'Me too,' said Alec.

DAT, DAT, DAT, DAT, DAT, DAT!

'Hannah, where are they?' pleaded Alec.

'I don't know. I can't sense them,' said Hannah.

'ARRRGGGHHHH!' screamed Terrence.

The purple wall swept over Terrence. He reached an arm out to Zach and disappeared.

Zach shook his head. 'I'm not going out like that.'

Alec held out his fist, 'Heroic charge?'

Zach hit his fist against Alec's, 'Hell, yes!'

Back in the concrete start room, Chris put her hand against her face as she watched her idiotic agents on the panel of smart-glass.

'Whoever runs the furthest wins,' called Hannah springing to her feet.

'CHARGE!' screamed Zach, blindly firing his weapon.

Alec raised his AR-15 to his shoulder and emptied his magazine as he ran.

DAT, DAT, DAT, DAT, DAT, CRACK, CRACK, CRACK, DAT, DAT, DAT, **DAT**, CRACK, CRACK, CRACK, CRACK, CRACK, CRACK, CRACK, CRACK, CRACK!

Hannah reached the other side of the park as music started playing. Alec and Zach were directly behind her. They hit the road and stopped.

'What's going on?' asked Alec.

Zach looked at the display on his arm. A bright yellow one was next to the words, Victory Royale.

'WE WON!' screamed Zach.

'Weeeeeehewwwww!' hollered Hannah.

The three of them starting dancing as the town disappeared and they were transported back into the start room. The other agents watching the battle on the panel of smart-glass embraced them, dancing and laughing with them until the music was replaced by the butler's voice.

'We'll you seem to be a bunch of happy bunnies. Eight began and three survive, that would clearly be cause for celebration. Where do I begin with this one? Some of my highlights were when an agent intentionally shot another agent, or what about when the team leader stood next to an open window in hostile territory and got killed or taking time out of a battle for a blossoming relationship or my personal favorite, the idiotic charge that ended in the luckiest shooting I've ever seen.'

A slow-motion clip of the trio's charge across the park in their bunny suits flashed onto the smart-glass. A camera followed the bullets fired by Alec that hit and killed two ninjas on the top of a roof top.

'They were wearing chaos crystals! That's why I couldn't sense them,' said Hannah.

The butler appeared once more. 'Thank you, Ruby for your services, you are being transferred to Mistopolis. You may go.'

Ruby vanished from the room.

The butler turned his gaze towards Hannah.

'Hannah, your gift is an asset to have in the field and it's clear to us you will see through the simulations we have prepared for the gifted students in Mistopolis unless we disable your gift which seems rather pointless. We have decided to place you within Bravo Two Eleven permanently if you agree with the transfer.

'I do,' said Hannah, smiling over at Ash.

'Very well, you'll conduct your agent training within the pods and join the team following graduation if you succeed. Goodbye.'

Hannah vanished.

The butler looked at Chris.

'I can see we have a lot of work to do to get your team to the level we expect you to be at before you leave. Babies must crawl before they walk, maybe so do you and your team. You won the Battle Royale, but it was through luck, not skill. Keep this up and I may have to restricted you to missions that have a difficulty rating of no higher than two.'

The butler faded off the screen and was replaced with words:

Health and ammunition restored.

Next simulation starts in 30 seconds.

M.I.S.T. Episode 3

Author: A.I. James

Episode 3.1

Health and ammunition restored.

Chris read the words on the smart glass panel as the rest of her team gathered around her inside the purple circle on the floor. The words on the screen faded. The mission parameters flashed onto the screen. Following each word were hundreds of possible answers shuffling within the answer box.

Fiona's voice emitted through the room from an unseen speaker. 'Please say stop when you are ready.'

Chris checked with her team. They all nodded.

'Stop!' said Chris.

The shuffling selections stopped.

Mission Type: Tactical Rescue

Map: Compound – Middle East

Uniform: Digital Camouflage

Weather: Midday / Sunny

Start Point: Safe House

Saving crystal enabled

Armory enabled

TOC support enabled

Healing Gift enabled

Difficulty 4/5

Chris and her team were suddenly dressed in digital camouflage with a Kevlar helmet and body armor.

Fiona appeared on the screen.

'Listen up Bravo Two Eleven, it's an immediate deployment. A compound is under attack. The compound is guarded by allied soldiers and houses humanitarian aid workers. International Security Forces are being deployed to reinforce the allied soldiers, but they're at least fifteen minutes out. There's report of heavy automatic gun fire and explosives. I've opened the nearest receiver, which is a safe house two blocks east of the compound. Choose your weapons and equipment from the armory. The armory tab will be disabled once you deploy. The mission will commence when you say, deploy now, but the longer you wait, the higher the likelihood the terrorists will kill the hostages and the mission will be a failure.'

'Can you answer any questions?' asked Chris.

'Of course.'

'How many terrorists?'

'I don't have that information. I do know that suicide bombers have breached the gates using two car bombs. It's in an unfriendly region so you may have to fight your way in.'

Chris turned to her team as she pushed the armory tab on the display strapped to her left arm. 'Assault Team, let's go M4's as our primary weapon, pistol as our secondary weapon. Plenty of grenades and Terrence, I want you carrying some breaching charges.' Each item Chris selected appeared on her the moment she pressed on it in her display. She turned to her sniper team. 'Ash and Owen, we might need your sniper rifles.'

'Already on it,' replied Ash, pressing equipment icons on his own display. His semi-automatic sniper rifle appeared in his left hand and an M4 with a grenade launcher was slung over his shoulder.

Chris looked at her team. Every agent had finished selecting items from the armory. 'Team, the second we arrive in the safe house, I want everyone checking the area in front of them for threats. Assault team has the lead to clear the safe house. Treat this like it's the real thing, not a game in a simulator. I want everyone coming back alive. Ready?'

'We're good, let's do this,' said Ash.

'DEPLOY NOW!' commanded Chris.

The floor dropped away in a rush. Chris and her team were standing inside a purple circle located inside the safe house. She searched her area of the room for threats. The room was dark and dusty and void of furniture. An open doorway led to a second room. The boarded-up windows to the street blocked most of the sunlight from entering the room. A shadow ran past the boarded window forcing Chris to turn instinctively towards the threat with her weapon, but whoever it was, they were outside, running past the safe house in the direction of the compound.

'Clear,' called Zach.

'Clear,' called Alec.

'Clear,' called Terrence.

'Room's clear,' confirmed Chris.

'Alec and Zach, check the back room. Terrence, cover the front door.'

Zach and Alec disappeared through the doorway. Seconds later, they were back in the room with their thumbs raised. The back room was clear.

Chris checked the map on her display and confirmed the route to the compound.

'Stack on the door,' ordered Chris.

The team stacked up against the wall beside the front door and waited for Chris's command to open the door and enter the street.

'Remember, our objective is to secure the compound. We can't get bogged down fighting in the street. Let's move out.'

Terrence yanked the door open and stepped aside as the team ran onto the street.

Chris squinted from the sun's glare. The air outside felt like she'd run into an oven. The hot wind lifted the top layer of dirt off the sunbaked road and formed a gritty paste in her mouth. To her left were buildings made from a mixture of mud and cement. To her right was a row of old, faded cars parked along the side of the road. Chris ignored the sweat beading down her forehead and ran along the sidewalk.

BOOM, BOOM, DAT, DAT, DAT, DAT, DAT!

The sounds of the fire-fight grew louder with every step Chris took towards the compound.

DAT, DAT!

'TAKE COVER!'

Chris dived behind the safety of a dirty, white sedan. She looked across the sidewalk to ensure her team wasn't injured. They were divided between those that instinctively dived to the shelter of the wall and those that launched themselves towards the nearest parked car as the two bullets slammed into the sidewalk.

'Where did that come from?' screamed Zach.

'It sounded like the rooftop across the street,' replied Terrence.

DAT, DAT, DAT, DAT, DAT!

Bullets sprayed the car Chris was using as cover. The car's shattered windows rained down over her.

Chris pushed her radio transmitter button.

'Assault team, on my command, provide covering fire at the rooftop. Snipers, when we start shooting, get into a position where you have eyes on that roof.'

'Copy that.'

'NOW!'

The assault team leapt from their cover and sprayed the rooftop with bullets.

CRACK, CRACK, CRACK, CRACK, CRACK, CRACK, CRACK, CRACK, CRACK, CRACK, CRACK, CRACK, CRACK, CRACK, CRACK, CRACK, CRACK, CRACK, CRACK, CRACK!

Ash and Owen moved into position to take an aimed shot.

'Owen, you've got the left side of the roof, I'll take the right side,' ordered Ash.

'Copy.'

The snipers scanned the rooftop for threats as the covering fire from the assault team slowed. Two heads cautiously popped up from behind the wall surrounding the rooftop. The snipers waited as the two men continued to rise, silhouetting themselves against the bright blue sky behind them. One man lifted an AK-47 over the wall whilst the other shouldered a rocket propelled grenade.

CRACK, CRACK!

The heads of the two men disintegrated from the sniper's bullets. The snipers scanned the rooftop for more threats.

'Are we clear?' asked Chris.

'We're clear,' confirmed Ash.

'Move out. The compound's just around the next corner,' said Chris.

The team stood up and continued down the street. Chris stopped with the rest of the team at the corner of the block. Her shoulders heaved under her body armor as her lungs fought to breathe in the thick warm air. The heat was draining the strength out of Chris at an alarming rate. She pointed at Ash and Owen and then pointed across the street to the parked flatbed truck.

Ash and Owen stood up and crossed the street, one at a time, whilst the assault team covered their movement.

Ash pushed the transmitting switch on his radio.

'Chris, we're in position.'

'Copy that. How does the compound look?'

'The gates are buckled and blown apart in the center. There are bodies on the street near the suicide bombers' cars. The cars are engulfed in flames. No signs of the allied soldiers that should be manning the bunkers on the corners of the compound.'

DAT, DAT, DAT, DAT, DAT, DAT, DAT, DAT, DAT!

Another long burst of automatic fire erupted from inside the compound.

'We're moving out. Snipers, are we clear?'

'You're clear.'

Chris stood up.

'Assault team, let's go.'

Chris led the team around the corner. They spread out across the street as they approached the compound. Charred and fragmented bodies littered the area. One was slowly clutching and pulling at the road, dragging his wounded body towards a safer area.

'Help...' begged the man, his voice made hoarse from the burns in his throat.

'Chris, do you want us to check the bodies?' asked Terrence.

'Negative, our priority is the compound. We'll come back for them after the aid workers are secure.'

The team ignored the pleas of the wounded and continued towards the buckled green gates of the compound. They were twenty yards from the gate when four gunmen rounded the corner of the street up ahead of them.

'Contact front,' bellowed Zach, raising his M4 to his shoulder.

CRACK, CRACK, CRACK, CRACK, **CRACK, CRACK,** CRACK!

A mixture of bullets from the assault and sniper teams decimated the group.

'Keep moving,' urged Chris.

They passed the gates and charged into the compound. A terrorist standing on the other side of a small, gravel car park raised his rifle to his shoulder.

CRACK, CRACK!

Terrence's double tap slammed the terrorist against the wall.

Chris examined the front section of the compound. In the corners of the front wall were sand-bagged gun posts. The allied soldiers who had been manning the gun posts at the time of the attack lay at the base of the ladders leading up to the posts, deceased from a mixture of burns and bullet wounds. In front of her was a two-level building with a flat roof that ran parallel to the car park and the front compound wall. The building wall facing the car park had no windows or doors for the aid workers protection. On both sides of the main building was an archway spanning the void to the single-story buildings that ran along the side walls of the compound. Chris quickly checked the compound map on her display to confirm she hadn't missed any entry points and noticed a stairwell from inside the main building leading to the roof.

Chris pushed her radio transmitter.

'Sniper team, get ready to move. Zach, cover the right archway. Terrence, cover the left archway. Alec, I want you in the right-side gun post,' said Chris as she ran to the gun post on the left.

The assault team scattered to their assigned areas. Chris looked around at her team. They were all in position. She pushed her radio transmitter.

'Sniper team, move to our location. Alec and I will cover you,' said Chris.

'Copy that,' replied Ash.

Ash and Owen left the cover of the truck and jogged down the exposed street towards the compound.

CRACK, CRACK!

'Tango down,' called Zach. 'I've got more coming.'

CRACK, CRACK, CRACK, CRACK, CRACK!

DAT, DAT, DAT, DAT, DAT, DAT, DAT!

'THEY'RE EVERYWHERE! I NEED SOME HELP,' warned Zach as more terrorists surged towards his location from deep inside the compound. 'TERRENCE, ARE YOU EVEN SHOOTING?'

CRACK, CRACK, CRACK, CRACK, CRACK, CRACK, CRACK, CRACK, CRACK, CRACK, CRACK, CRACK, CRACK, CRACK, CRACK!

Chris turned. Zach and Terrence were firing as fast as they could pull their triggers. She pushed her radio transmitter. 'Alec, I'll cover the sniper team, go help out Zach.'

'Copy that.'

Chris looked back down the street past the snipers and instantly pushed her radio transmitter.

'Sniper team, keep running, you've got a vehicle-mounted group on your six!' warned Chris.

Chris released her weapon and grasped the heavy machine gun resting on the sand bags in front of her. She yanked back on the cocking handle, aimed at the vehicle's fuel tank and squeezed the trigger all the way back.

CRACK, CRACK, CRACK, CRACK, CRACK, CRACK, CRACK, CRACK, CRACK, CRACK, CRACK, BOOM!

The vehicle and its occupants disappeared inside the orange fireball. Ash and Owen turned into the gates and ran inside the compound.

'Chris, where do you want us?' asked Ash.

'Ash, swap out with me. Owen, I want you in the other gun post. We need to locate the aid workers.'

Chris descended the ladder of the gun post and knelt against the compound wall. She pushed the crystal on the map of her display until the pop-up text box appeared. She pressed retrieve and held out her hand. She caught the crystal as it flew towards her and immediately activated it. She ran over to Alec and Zach and peered around the corner into the compound. Half a dozen bodies of the allied security team lay where they fell from the terrorist's bullets. There was a door to the ground level to the main building five yards from each archway. Terrence was visible at the other archway, on one knee, firing at will, at the terrorists inside the compound.

CRACK, CRACK...CRACK, CRACK...CRACK, CRACK!

'I'm almost out,' warned Terrence as another terrorist collapsed to the ground.

Chris tapped Zach's shoulder. 'Go back around the front of the building and meet up with Terrence.' She pushed her radio pressure switch. 'Terrence, I'm sending Zach to your location. He's coming from the front of the compound, so don't shoot him.'

'Copy that,' said Terrence, releasing his M4 and drawing his pistol from his thigh holster as he continued firing.

CRACK,   CRACK.....................CRACK, CRACK...CRACK, CRACK!

A terrorist on the other side of an open grassed area stepped out of his concealed position and cocked his arm back to throw a grenade. Chris raised her M4, quickly centered the red dot within her scope over his chest and squeezed the trigger.

CRACK!

The terrorist twisted violently to his right and spun through the air with the grace of an untrained gymnast. He slammed into the wall behind him. The grenade fell to his side and exploded.

BOOM!

Fragments of shrapnel and body parts flew in every direction.

'Cover me,' requested Terrence as Zach approached him.

'Covering,' confirmed Zach, stepping up to Terrence's shoulder to protect him while he had his head down.

Terrence flicked the magazine release of his pistol with his thumb, slammed a full clip inside the pistol and released the slide. He then reloaded his M4.

'Coming up,' said Terrence, holstering his pistol and raising his M4 to re-enter the fight but the terrorists had stopped attacking. If there were any left inside the compound, they were either hiding or dead.

'Chris, this is Fiona. I've just been advised there's a safe room inside the building that runs along the western wall of the compound. If the aid workers had enough time, that's where you'll find them. I'm sending the data to your display.'

'Thanks, Fi. Copy that.'

Chris checked the map on her display. A small blue dot was now flashing in the building at the other end of the compound. She looked up and examined the interior of the compound. In front of her was an open grassed area the size of a basketball court. Grey concrete buildings bordered the grass on every side. The main building within the compound to her left was the only double-story building. The remaining buildings bordering the grassed area mirrored each other with a walled balcony and large open windows. The rooms within the buildings were set back behind the balcony wall. Chris pushed her radio transmitter.

'Listen up team, we're going to clear both levels of the main building in a simultaneous room entry and then push towards the western building where the safe room is located. Alec and Terrence, when we go in, have a cooked stun grenade ready to deploy. Snipers, stay outside and provide cover while we clear the building. Once we've cleared the main building, I want Ash to set up inside the second level of the main building to give us covering fire. Owen, I want you to move first and set-up on the roof to cover the street.'

'Copy,' replied Ash and Owen.

'Copy,' replied Zach and Terrence.

Alec reached into the front pouch on his body armor and removed a stun grenade. He placed the lever of the grenade inside the palm of his right hand, slid his left index finger into the ring attached to the pin and waited for Chris's command.

'All call signs, ready-'

Alec pulled the pin out of the top of the grenade.

'Standby-'

Alec released the grip of the grenade, allowing the lever to spring back. The grenade was armed. He continued to hold the grenade that was seconds away from exploding.

'GO, GO, GO!'

Alec ran out of the safety of the archway and closed in on the door. Forty yards along the balcony, Terrence ran with the same urgency to get rid of the cooked grenade. Alec grasped the door handle. He yanked the door open and hurled the stun grenade inside.

BOOM!

Fragments of bright orange and yellow metal scattered throughout the room as Chris ran inside. She scanned the room from left to right, her body moving back and forth behind her M4 as though it were an extension of her own body. The room was clear. Gunfire erupted from the room Zach and Terrence were clearing. Chris ran to the back wall of the dark room and entered the stairway that led to the second level. She sprinted up the stairs.

Chris entered the room at the top of the stairs and turned to the right as Alec turned to the left. Three men were standing behind a female aid worker. A male aid worker lay motionless on the floor five yards away from the woman with blood dripping out of his ears and mouth.

CRACK, CRACK, CRACK, CRACK, CRACK!

Only one of the men was quick enough to raise his rifle before Chris and Alec started firing. All three collapsed to the floor. Chris saw movement at the other side of the room. She aimed her M4 towards the threat. Zach and Terrence entered the room and split off to each side of the doorway, mirroring Chris and Alec's movement seconds earlier. Two of Zach's throwing knives were missing from his forearm guards.

Chris rushed to the woman and knelt beside her.

'We're a 10 Regiment team. You're safe now.'

'Thank you. Thank you so much. They were going to-'

'I know. It's okay, you're safe now,' repeated Chris. She placed a reassuring hand onto the woman's shoulder to calm her.

'Alec, check the other hostage,' ordered Chris.

Alec moved to the man's side and performed a quick assessment.

'He's alive, but unconscious, strong pulse, regular breathing, and a dilated right eye.'

'Fi, this is Chris. We've located two hostages, level two in the eastern building,' reported Chris.

'Acknowledged, I confirm two hostages. What's their status?' asked Fiona.

'One is shaken up but uninjured; the other is unconscious with a serious head injury. I'm moving Owen to work on him.'

'Copy that. I'll notify command and order a medical helicopter when the area is secure,' replied Fiona.

'Chris, I got clipped in the room entry,' said Zach, kneeling next to the door he entered through. He checked his health bar on his display which had dropped from green to almost the bottom of the yellow zone. 'I'm going to need Owen in the next three to five minutes.'

Chris looked over at Zach. Two bullet holes in the left sleeve of his shirt were oozing blood. He had his right hand over a wound on his left shoulder that was spurting blood through his fingers.

'Terrence, wrap some dressings around his wounds to slow the bleeding,' said Chris.

'Sniper team, report,' ordered Chris.

'It's quiet down here,' replied Ash.

'Copy that. Owen, move to our location,' said Chris.

'Chris, this is Fiona, the reinforcements are approximately six minutes out from your location.'

'Thanks, Fi.'

Owen entered the room.

Chris pointed at Zach. 'Zach first, then the man. Give your sniper rifle to Terrence. Alec, take Terrence and confirm the roof top is clear. Terrence, you'll be staying up there and covering the street.'

'On it,' said Alec, running towards the internal staircase that led to the roof.

Owen's hands began glowing the soft blue color of his healing gift as he approached Zach. He knelt next to him and placed his hands over Zach's arm and shoulder. He gave just enough of his gift to fill up Zach's health bar on his display before he moved onto the unconscious man.

'Chris, this is Alec, roof is clear.'

'Copy that, Alec and Ash, come to my location. Terrence, take up a position to cover the street. Reinforcements are five minutes out.'

Ash entered the room shortly after Alec.

Chris pointed at the wall of the inner compound. 'Ash, I want you by that window overlooking the compound. Assault team, fall in on me,' ordered Chris. She waited for her team to huddle around her before issuing her next command. 'We need to get to the western building. Zach, you take the northern building. Alec and I will take the southern building and we'll meet up at the safe room.'

'Do you want to move the crystal?' asked Alec.

'Yep, good call,' said Chris, pushing the crystal on the map of her display until the pop-up text box appeared. She pressed retrieve and held out her hand. She caught the crystal and activated it in the middle of the room.

Chris moved to the door on the opposite side of the room and descended the stairs to the ground level. A man with two throwing knives lodged in his throat lay lifeless at the base of the stairs; blood pooled on the floor around his head. The heat had already caused the outer edges of the blood to congeal. Evidence of Zach and Terrence's fight to clear the room was plain to see. Bullet holes pitted the cement walls at random intervals and seven bodies lay in the far corner. The black scorched mark from where the stun grenade ignited had landed right next to the first man's foot and the acrid smell of gun powder and magnesium hung in the air.

Chris stole a quick glance out of the door at the silent compound. There was zero movement. She stepped outside and cautiously moved onto the grassed area towards the cement balcony on the southern building. She stepped onto the balcony and into the shade. Bodies littered the floor below the open windows where the terrorists had fallen victim to her team's bullets. As she reached each window in the interior wall, she conducted a quick search of the room and continued moving. Her priority was reaching the safe room and securing the hostages. She edged towards the last window in the building when she heard the unmistakable noise of a rocket-propelled grenade ripping through the air.

SWOOOOOOOOSH!

'RPG, TAKE COVER,' screamed Chris.

The small rocket left a trail of smoke like a meteorite as it flew over the roof of her building and slammed into the balcony wall of the northern building.

BOOM!

DAT, DAT, DAT, DAT, DAT, DAT, DAT, DAT, DAT, DAT, DAT, DAT, DAT, DAT, DAT, DAT, DAT, DAT, DAT, DAT, DAT, DAT, DAT, DAT, DAT, DAT!

SWOOOOOOOOSH!

'Another RPG,' warned Ash's voice through Chris's ear piece.

BOOM!

Half of the balcony collapsed. The crumbling walls threw a cloud of cement dust into the air.

'ZACH ARE YOU HIT?' asked Chris.

'A piece of shrapnel missed my junk by two inches,' declared Zach. 'I've lost a quarter of my health bar. I swear this mission is cursed.'

'Have you got cover?' asked Chris.

'I can hold out here,' replied Zach.

CRACK, CRACK, CRACK, CRACK, CRACK, CRACK, CRACK, CRACK!

Ash and Terrence unleashed a volley of bullets into the abandoned-looking building that towered over the southern wall of the compound on the opposite side of the street.

DAT, DAT, DAT, DAT, DAT, DAT, DAT, DAT, DAT, DAT, DAT, DAT, DAT!

'Ash, have you got their location?' asked Chris.

'They're in a building past the southern wall. They're on the forth level, but they're too deep into the room. I can't see anything but the light from their muzzle flash.'

Ash fired another short burst.

CRACK, CRACK, CRACK, CRACK, CRACK!

SWOOOOOOOOOSH!

'CHRIS, RPG COMING YOUR WAY. TAKE COVER!' warned Ash as another RPG flew towards the compound.

BOOM!

The roof above Chris caved in. Alec lifted a block of cement off Chris's waist and pulled her up to her knees.

'Are you okay?' asked Alec.

Chris looked at her display. She'd lost three quarters of her health bar.

'I'll live.'

Chris pushed her radio pressure switch.

'Fi, this is Chris, have we got any air support?'

'Negative. We can send up our own drones, but the closest receiver it could deploy from is twenty minutes flight time from you.'

'Ash, can you get a field receiver into the building?' asked Chris.

'Yeah, but they've got the window heavily sandbagged. It will have to be on the level below them.'

'Do it. I'll set one up here. We'll go to them.'

'Copy that.'

'Fi, this is Chris, I'm setting up a field receiver; Ash is shooting one into the building. I want you to co-ordinate the server link with Ash's shot, so we take them by surprise.' Chris pulled the receiver out of the pouch on the front of her body armor and read the number on its side. 'Fi, my field receiver code is FR296.' She flicked open the safety cap on the top of the receiver with her thumb and pushed the button in and waited.

BEEP!

She tossed it into the corner of the balcony. Black light spread out of the receiver like a torch beam. The shadowy mass curved at the edges in a clockwise direction, gaining speed with every revolution it completed.

'Fi, this is Chris. My wormhole is active. Zach, we're taking care of the threat. Sit tight and stay hidden,' said Chris.

'Fi, this is Ash. My field receiver code is FR322. I'm ready to take the shot. Let me know when you are ready to connect the link.'

'I'm ready and waiting for the command,' replied Fiona, punching the code of Ash's field receiver into her keyboard.

'Copy that. Stand by,' said Ash. He slid the 40mm projectile with the field receiver inside it into the barrel of the grenade launcher. He lifted the butt of the M4 to his shoulder and stared at the third-level window through the scope.

Chris and Alec reloaded their M4s and waited for Ash's shot.

Ash took a deep breath in and exhaled slightly. He squeezed the trigger.

CRACK!

The field receiver spiraled through the air and disappeared through the window.

'That's a good shot,' reported Ash.

'Wormhole is active and the server link is secure,' said Fiona.

'Copy that,' said Chris, running into the wormhole with Alec by her side.

Chris stepped out of the wormhole and scanned for threats to her left as Alec did the same to the right.

'Left clear,' whispered Chris.

'Right clear,' whispered Alec.

DAT, DAT, DAT, DAT, DAT, DAT, DAT, DAT, DAT!

CRACK, CRACK, CRACK, CRACK!

The noise from both the machine gun on the level above her and the impact of Ash's return fire was deafening. Chris ran to the entrance of the stairwell at the back of the abandoned level. Every second she wasted was another second the group above her could shoot at her team and potentially kill them. She entered the enclosed stairwell and climbed the steps. She rounded the corner of the landing between the two levels and ran into the side of a barrel-chested man. Chris smashed the butt of her M4 across his cheek, knocking the man down. His head slammed into the edge of the concrete step.

DAT, DAT, DAT, DAT, DAT, DAT, DAT!

Another burst erupted from the machine gun beyond the door on the next level.

Chris slammed her left boot onto the dazed man's throat, cutting off his air supply, making it impossible for the man to scream for help. His eyes bulged as she pointed the barrel of her weapon at his forehead.

DAT, CRACK, **DAT, DAT, DAT, DAT, DAT!**

The noise from the machine gun concealed her shot. The man's body went limp under Chris's boot. She removed her foot and continued up the stairs.

'Cover me,' she whispered.

Alec nodded and stepped to the side of the plain wooden door with his weapon focused on the door handle. Chris knelt next to the door and removed her snake camera from the pouch on her body armor. She turned on the hand-held screen and fed the flexible camera tube into the gap between the door and the floor. There were two men inside the room. One man was positioned next to the gun and the second man stood behind the gunner with an RPG in his hands. Both were standing near the hole in the sandbagged window. She turned the camera left and right. A dozen RPGs were piled up near the wall to the left of the door. Below the machine gun was a stack of two-hundred-round belts of ammunition. She took a final look around the room and pulled back the camera tube. She turned to Alec and used hand signals to relay the position of the two men inside the room. Alec raised his thumb.

Chris turned the door handle, but it didn't budge. The door was locked. She stepped back one pace, raised her foot and kicked the door with every ounce of strength she possessed. Her leg jarred from the impact even though the door frame splintered in four different sections. She raised her weapon as the door swung open and followed Alec into the room.

CRACK, CRACK!

The machine gunner slumped forward over the top of the gun as most of his head continued with the two bullets through the window.

'DON'T DO IT,' warned Chris as the man holding the RPG raised it towards her.

CRACK, CRACK, CRACK, CRACK, CRACK!

The combined single shots from Chris and the spray of bullets from Alec's weapon ripped the man's chest apart. The RPG hit the floor immediately before the man's body.

'Bravo Two Eleven, this is Chris. Terrorist room secured.'

'Copy that, Chris. I'm moving to the safe room,' replied Zach.

'Copy that,' replied Chris.

Chris pulled the gun off the sandbagged window and stripped it down until she could get to the firing pin. She pulled it out and slipped it into her body armor to prevent anyone else using the gun. Alec helped her carry the machine gun parts and the remaining belts of ammunition over to the pile of RPGs. They dumped them on the floor and each removed two high-explosive grenades from their body armor.

'Team, this is Chris. Be advised, we are blowing the remaining weapons within the room.'

She pulled the pins from her grenades as Alec did the same. They lowered the grenades into the pile of weapons and sprinted towards the door. They'd made it down the flight of stairs and back inside the third level by the time the grenades exploded.

BOOM!

The room shuddered as Chris and Alec dived into the safety of the black wormhole. They exited the wormhole onto the balcony and slammed into the false wall just in time to feel the full effect of the shockwave from the RPGs exploding.

'Fi, detonate the field receiver inside the building,' ordered Chris.

BOOM!

'Field receiver is terminated,' confirmed Fiona.

Chris got to her feet and collected the field receiver she had used. She deactivated the switch and slid it back into its pouch on her body armor. She began to move towards the northern building just as Zach reported in over the radio.

'TOC, this is Zach. Twelve hostages located within the safe room with no injuries to report.'

'I have a visual on the reinforcement soldiers,' reported Terrence.

'Copy that,' said Chris.

'Ash, raise the flag,' ordered Chris.

Ash walked to the flag pole at the front of the compound. He removed the black flag with the 10 Regiment logo from the pouch on his body armor and attached it to the rope, before raising it to the top of the flag pole and securing it.

Chris and Alec assisted Zach in guiding the hostages out onto the grassed area as Owen escorted the two aid workers from the main building onto the grass. The team took up a defensive position on each corner of the field in case any more surprises occurred. Chris knelt at the south-west corner of the field and quickly glanced around the compound at the carnage her team had caused.

'Here they come,' said Chris as the first allied soldier walked through the archway and onto the grass of the inner compound.

Chris's vision blurred. She closed her eyes as her body swayed. The vertigo feeling stopped. She opened her eyes slowly. She was back inside the concrete room with the rest of her team. The bald butler dressed in a tuxedo appeared on the panel of smart-glass.

'Your mission was a success. I have no doubt that you're as shocked as I am. In future missions, remember the field receivers aren't only a last resort measure for neutralizing a hostile enemy, they can also be deployed for rapid movement through hostile territory,'

The butler faded off the screen and was replaced with words:

Health restored.

Next simulation starts in 30 seconds.

Other 10 Regiment Studios Books

Bravo Two Eleven, Origins, Part 1 / Part 2

Part One Release - September 29, 2018; Word Count: 104,714
Part Two Release - September 29, 2018; Word Count: 34,477
Written by: A.I. James
Style: Novel

Description: Christine Whittaker, or Chris, as she's known by her family and friends, has no idea she is living inside a computer game and when the game developers alter the game, Chris's entire world can be created, changed or taken away in an instant.

Chris awakes in a school classroom with a tragic backstory and her immediate future looks as bleak as her past. Chris discovers she is one of seventy high school students within the Allied Countries to be recommended for selection testing as an elite agent in the male-only 10 Regiment, but Chris was never meant to be selected. Every candidate with a girl's name was automatically rejected. Chris attends selection testing against all odds and when not one, but two boys are attracted to her, she must choose what's more important to her - being loved as she's always dreamed of from Alec or Ash, or a career she never knew existed and the fate of the world.

Was Chris's selection 10 Regiment's mistake or her destiny?

Will Chris blaze a new trail or go down in flames?

Sometimes, the fate of the world rests with the people who were never meant to be in the spotlight...even those that are less than a day old!

10 Regiment Website

10 Regiment Studios specialize in tactical stories which also include superhero elements at times.

10 Regiment Studios has two series:

- Fortnite Battle Royale: Stories of gamers deploying inside the world of Fortnite Battle Royale using 10 Regiment's M.I.S.T. Pods technology.

-

- Bravo Two Eleven: This is our own original storyline about characters who don't know they exist inside a computer game and the game developers have no idea how every change or update they publish impacts the characters and the world inside the game. This series blends the best of games like Fortnite and Call of Duty with the magic and superpowers from Marvel. The M.I.S.T. books are an ongoing series filled with action packed mission deployments and bonus features. The Bravo Two Eleven Origins novel is a completed story with deeper character development and storylines that follows the character's journey from school students to elite agents. The first three stories within the book, Bravo Two Eleven M.I.S.T. Season 1 are available at the back of this book as free bonus features for your reading pleasure.

Join the free Agent List if you want to know when a new book is coming and if you want to get one free randomly selected story from every new Bravo Two Eleven M.I.S.T. book to beta test read before it is published. Give feedback to the author and help guide the direction of the series. If you sign up now, you'll get one story from Bravo Two Eleven, M.I.S.T. Season 1 within the first 72 hours of becoming an agent. 10 Regiment Studios also has a Free-to-Read or Buy-to-Binge mission. To find out more, go to:

www.10regiment.com

Credits

Fortnite Battle Royale: The next evolution, Volume 1

Author: A.I. James

Publisher: 10 Regiment Studios

Creator / Author / Director

Andrew holds a Bachelor-in-Clinical Practice (Paramedic) and has completed many courses in prehospital medicine and emergency response. Andrew has attended masterclasses in Fantasy writing and editing and has also completed several short courses in writing for children and young adults.

Andrew served thirteen years in the Medical Corps in the Australian Army and discharged with the rank of Sergeant in 2007. He was posted to units specializing in infantry, bomb disposal, construction and Special Forces. It was among the Special Forces that Andrew felt most content. He is skilled in various infantry/Special Forces weapons and techniques such as: assault rifles, sub-machine guns, pistols and grenades; roping in an urban environment, natural environment, and out of helicopters; team insertion by foot, Armored Personnel Carrier, Helicopters and Amphibious Operations; team, platoon, company and battalion tactics for remote patrols and urban Counter-Terrorism; and Advanced Cardiac and Trauma Life Support.

Andrew utilized this training to great benefit during the seven-month deployment to Batagade, East Timor, also during the four years he spent with the Commando Regiment. Two of those years were served in the Counter Terrorist Team – Tactical Assault Group – East (TAG-E). Andrew has been awarded the Australian Active Service Medal, the United Nations Medal, the Defense Force Medal and an Exemplary Service Medallion for stabilizing casualties with life-threatening injuries.

He now works as an Offshore Paramedic on oil rigs and gas platforms, which gives him plenty of time to deploy with the characters in his imagination.

Copyright

Made in the USA
Columbia, SC
10 December 2018